This is the eleventh volume of Charlie Small's amazing journal.

A family found it on their camping holiday in the wilds of the West Country. They were out rambling one day when they came across the ashes of an old campfire; wedged under a nearby stone was this book. It was dirty and covered in ash, but one look inside showed they had discovered a brand new Charlie Small journal. It was packed with tales of incredible adventures, and as soon as the family got back from their trip they posted it to us. Here is the most exciting Charlie Small book so far!

There must be other notebooks to find, so keep your eyes peeled. If you do come across a curious-looking diary, or see an eight-year-old boy wearing a battered rucksack and riding a strange scooter with no wheels, please let us know at the website: **www.charliesmall.co.uk**

Mr Nickelodious
Trumpery Ward

GENTLEMAN EXPLORER AND
CUSTODIAN OF THE CHARLIE SMALL JOURNALS

This is the only known photograph of
Charlie Small in existence

Yum Yum!

Wurtbogs are stupid! true.

THE AMAZING ADVENTURES OF CHARLIE SMALL (400)

Notebook 11

THE HAWK'S NEST

↑ Thorn from the nest — actual size

CHARLIE SMALL JOURNAL 11: THE HAWK'S NEST
A RED FOX BOOK 978 1 782 95330 2

First published in Great Britain by David Fickling Books,
previously an imprint of Random House Children's Publishers UK
A Penguin Random House Company

This Red Fox edition published 2014

5 7 9 10 8 6 4

Text and illustrations copyright © Charlie Small, 2011

Penguin Random House is committed to a sustainable future for
our business, our readers and our planet. This book is made from
Forest Stewardship Council® certified paper.

Printed and bound in Great Britain by Clays Ltd, Elcograf S.p.A.

Set in 15/17pt Garamond MT

Red Fox Books are published by Random House Children's Publishers UK,
61–63 Uxbridge Road, London W5 5SA

www.**randomhousechildrens**.co.uk
www.**totallyrandombooks**.co.uk
www.**randomhouse**.co.uk

Addresses for companies within The Random House Group Limited can be found at:
www.**randomhouse**.co.uk/offices.htm

THE RANDOM HOUSE GROUP Limited Reg. No. 954009

A CIP catalogue record for this book is available from the British Library.

NAME: Charlie Small

ADDRESS: The Hawk's Nest, Darkmoor!

AGE: I'm a four-hundred-year-old boy!

MOBILE: 07713 12 5

SCHOOL: The school of adventure!

THINGS I LIKE: Jakeman and Philly; the Air-rider; Moor Folk; The Hawk

THINGS I HATE: Joseph Craik (my arch enemy); every last one of his lousy gang; Wartbogs; foul-smelling quagmires

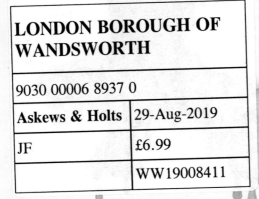

If you find this book, PLEASE look after it. This is the ONLY true account of my remarkable adventures.

My name is Charlie Small and I am four-hundred years old, maybe even more. But in all those long years, I have never grown up. Something happened when I was eight years old, something I can't begin to understand. I went on a journey... and I'm still trying to find my way home. Now, although I've ridden across ~~contine~~ continents on a flying scooter, been chased by brainless Wartbogs and was nearly sucked beneath Gloopen Mire, I still look like any eight-year-old boy you might pass in the street.

I've crossed storm-tossed seas, buried a skeletal pirate and joined forces with the mysterious Hawk. You may think this sounds fantastic; you could think it's a lie, but you would be wrong. Because EVERYTHING IN THIS BOOK IS TRUE. Believe this single fact and you can share the most incredible journey ever experienced.

Charlie Small

Safe At Last!

'Home!' cried Jakeman as his Factory of Marvellous Inventions came into view. 'Hoo-bloomin-ray! I thought we'd never get here.'

The long, gabled building with five tall chimneys was in darkness, apart from a single light above the entrance gates.

'I need a cup of hot, sweet tea,' groaned Harmonia.

'And I need my bed,' whimpered my best friend, Philly. 'My feet are killing me.'

'I'm not surprised. We must have walked a hundred miles!' I groaned. But at least we were safe. Only a few days ago, it had looked like our number was up!

Blown From The Sky!

Four days earlier, my pal Jakeman, his granddaughter Philly and her mum and dad had rescued me from an enormous, dinosaur-infested gaming stadium. We didn't get far in their incredible space balloon before the master of the stadium attacked: Nemesis Gamer flew from the clouds on a bat-winged microlight, firing air-to-air missiles. *Boof! Boof! Boof!* Our balloon was hit and we plummeted earthwards.

'Hold on to your hats,' cried Jakeman, pulling a lever to jettison the deflated balloon that flapped uselessly above our capsule. The freed balloon flew across the sky and wrapped itself around Gamer's aircraft.

'Drat!' Gamer yelled as he spiralled down like a swatted fly, leaping from the mini-plane at the last minute and opening a parachute.

Jakeman pressed a button on our capsule's dashboard and a triangular wing opened out on each side of the pod. We glided out of our fall, swooped across the surrounding countryside and landed

We glided out of our fall

(See my Journal Land Of The Remotosaurs)

in a distant field. It was only when we crawled from the dented machine that we discovered the field was home to a *very* bad-tempered bull.

It pawed the ground, snorted a cloud of steam from its twitching nostrils and charged straight towards Jakeman. The inventor was bending over to inspect a rare plant, offering the bellowing beast a perfect target.

'Watch your bottom!' I yelled.

Jakeman looked round.

'Yikes!' he cried as the bull thundered towards him – and he shot off at a surprising speed for such a rickety old man. He cleared a five-bar gate in one spectacular bound and landed face down in a deep and dirty puddle!

The bull charged!

The Long Walk

Poor old Jakeman was soaked through, and moaned and groaned for the rest of the day as we headed across the countryside towards his factory. He wasn't the only one! Philly was all right, but you'd have thought her mum and dad, Harmonia and Theo, had been brought up in a palace rather than spending the last five years below ground on a distant and dangerous planet!

As we tramped through the afternoon, the complaints grew worse. Harmonia was too cold; Theo was too warm; Jakeman's damp trousers were making his legs sore. They were all hungry, they were thirsty, their feet were hurting and the sun was giving them headaches. Philly looked at me, raised her eyes and shook her head in disbelief. It was like looking after a bunch of toddlers!

'OK, we'll make camp as soon as we find a decent spot,' I sighed. Being an experienced explorer, I was used to surviving in the wild and began picking berries from hedgerows and digging up root vegetables from fields as we walked. Finally, we came to a flat area of grass

(See my journal Planet of The Gerks!)

protected on all sides by high hedges.

'This'll do,' I said, and the grown-ups collapsed in exhausted heaps as Philly and I went off to collect firewood. Within a quarter of an hour, we had a fire burning and I started to prepare supper.

'You don't expect us to eat these do you?' gasped Jakeman, holding up a gnarled and dirty turnip. 'I mean – they've been in the ground with worms crawling all over them!'

'*You* don't have to eat any,' I said, packing a layer of mud around the turnips and throwing them onto the fire. 'But you'll be missing a treat. It's an old forest recipe taught to me by Bella, a ferocious female member of the Special Badger Service.'

We waited an hour for the turnips to bake through, then I flicked from them the ashes with a stick and cracked open the casing of hardened mud. Inside, the vegetables were soft and fragrant and a delicious smell wafted into the night air.

(see my journal Forest Of skulls)

Bella of the SBS

'OK, I'll give it a go,' said Jakeman as I passed them round and, after a tentative nibble, he wolfed his down in record time. 'Mmm, not bad. Have you got any more?' he asked.

We ate a hearty meal, but if I thought the moaning was over I was wrong, as I discovered when I pointed out the best place to sleep.

'In a *ditch*?' cried Harmonia.

'There's no better place if it's nice and dry,' I explained. 'I've done it loads of times. You'll be out of the wind; you can line the bottom with dried grasses and cover yourselves with leaves. You won't believe how warm and comfy you'll be.'

After much grumbling, Philly and I got everyone settled in a line along the ditch.

'I won't sleep a wink, I know I won't,' said Harmonia, but within two minutes she was snoring loudly.

Jakeman Has Plans For Me!

She was still out cold when Philly and I began preparing a breakfast of sweet berries the following morning.

'Sleep all right, Mum?' asked Philly, with a wicked twinkle in her eye, as Harmonia finally crawled out of the ditch, her hair a tangle of grass and straw.

'I didn't close my eyes for a minute,' replied Harmonia. 'I've never *been* so uncomfortable!' And we all burst out laughing.

We carried on with our journey, following the compass in my explorer's kit towards Jakeman's factory. That night we slept in a haystack; the night after in a dry recess behind the curtain of water made by a high waterfall. Eventually, at the end of the fourth day, Jakeman's Factory came into view and we breathed a collective sigh of relief!

As soon as we got inside, we had a slap-up meal of bacon, eggs, chips and beans. That's when Jakeman told me an incredible and momentous piece of news.

'Tomorrow, once I've checked the Archway To Anywhere machine, I will be able to send you home for your tea, Charlie,' he beamed through a mouthful of chips.

I will be able to send you home for your tea, Charlie

YIPPEE! I've heard so much about this wonderful machine that will transport me back to my own world, and I'm *finally* going to try it out. I can hardly wait.

We are so tired that we've left the washing-up until morning, and now we are all safely tucked up in bed. I'm in the same room as the last time I stayed at the factory but I just can't get to sleep, despite being in a proper bed for the first time in an age.

I have tossed and turned, remembering all my crazy adventures and thinking about going home to Mum and Dad and my schoolmates. I'm feeling excited and miserable at the same time, because I really want to get home again, but I'm also *really* enjoying exploring this wonderful world.

I've switched the light back on now. If I can't sleep I might as well write up my journal. Who knows, this may be the last entry I make before I get home. Oh well, let's wait and see what tomorrow brings. I am feeling sleepy now, and think I might be able to drop off to . . .

Waiting And Waiting...

The next morning I was like a cat on hot bricks, waiting for Jakeman to check the transporting machine before sending me home.

Philly was very quiet and rather sulky. I don't think she wants me to go – or perhaps she isn't quite as confident about the Archway To Anywhere as her grandpa. I'm not surprised – it just looks like a big metal doorframe with a load of wires attached to it. Standing in front of the archway is an enormous and ancient-looking cannon.

Finally, Jakeman stopped fiddling with electrodes, calculators and prisms, and announced it was time to do a test run.

'And here is our fearless test-pilot,' he said, producing a very scruffy teddy bear from behind his back.

'Hey, you can't use Snozzle!' cried Philly. 'I've had him since I was two.'

'Oh, Philly, that bear has been in a box for the last five years' said Jakeman.

'Yeah, but – oh, OK,' said Philly reluctantly. 'We'd better make sure everything works before you send Charlie off into the ether!'

'Exactly so,' beamed Jakeman and dropped the teddy down the barrel of the cannon.

'So, what happens, exactly?' I asked, feeling nervous for the first time.

'Well, it's quite fascinating really, but very complicated,' said Jakeman breezily. 'I fire up the archway, which is really a huge electro-magnet that's so powerful it can break matter down into atoms. Then I blast you out of the cannon at exactly the right velocity. Too powerful a charge and you'd shoot through your world and end up somewhere else altogether!'

'You're kidding, right?' I said, my mouth

open in disbelief.

'Don't look so scared, Charlie,' said Jakeman, and continued with his explanation. 'So, passing through the arch at the right speed, you are evaporated and an instant later will reform in your own world. Simple!'

'You're sure the atoms come back together in my world, right?' I said, feeling even more nervous about my impending trip.

'Yes, absolutely,' said Jakeman, looking slightly shifty.

'And you have proof of that?' I asked, imagining my atoms floating through space for eternity.

'Well, not proof exactly,' said Jakeman. 'I couldn't get proof without transporting *myself* to your world and then I might never get back. But you're worrying about nothing, Charlie. If all my calculations are correct, I'm sure you will reform in your own world. Now, stand back everyone and be amazed!'

Barbequed!!

We stood back as Jakeman turned a big dial on the archway and a faint humming started up. The humming got louder and louder and the arch started to vibrate violently. Soon we couldn't hear ourselves speak.

'Wait for it, wait for it,' yelled Jakeman above the din and just as I thought my eardrums would burst, he flicked a switch, the cannon roared and poor Snozzle went shooting out of the end at a hundred miles an hour! As he passed under the archway there was a flash of bright light that blinded us all for a moment and left spots floating before my eyes. Then, as my vision cleared I looked to see if the teddy had disappeared.

'NO!' I cried. I couldn't believe it. After all my waiting and hoping, I'd been let down at the last hurdle.

'Oh my goodness,' said Jakeman, picking up the frazzled remains of the ancient teddy bear. 'I don't understand. It seemed to work when I tried it on a cockroach. Let me tweak a few buttons, I'm sure it'll be OK.'

'No *way* am I going to risk being transported in that,' I said, horrified. Philly's favourite toy had been reduced to a pile of smoking ashes!

'Don't worry, I *will* get you home, Charlie,' said Jakeman, looking very concerned. 'After all, it was one of my experiments that brought you here in the first place.'

'Really?' I said. I wasn't surprised. Jakeman had hinted in the past that he might have had something to do with it.

'Yes,' said Jakeman looking bashful. 'You see, I am convinced the universe is made up of layers of parallel worlds and I was sure I could break down the barriers between them with my Super-duper Laser Projector. Its beam is so powerful it can rip through time and space, but it needs a huge electric charge to power it; so one stormy night I raised a tall lightning conductor on top of the big clock on my factory roof. As the storm broke, a massive bolt of lightning hit the conductor and *WHAM!* A laser beam went streaking across the sky.'

'What happened next?' I asked.

'The storm grew worse. Clouds boiled in the sky, coloured lights flashed and thunderclaps crashed across the heavens. I knew that *somewhere* I had succeeded in bridging two worlds,' continued Jakeman, his eyes shining with excitement.

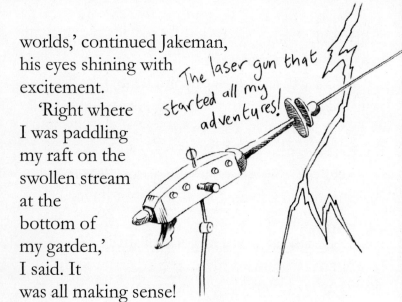

The laser gun that started all my adventures!

'Right where I was paddling my raft on the swollen stream at the bottom of my garden,' I said. It was all making sense!

'So it would seem, Charlie,' said Jakeman. 'And you sailed through into this world. I immediately picked you up on my radar system.'

'And now you can't get me back home,' I said crossly. 'Thanks a million.'

'You never told me about someone coming from another world,' said Philly crossing her arms and staring hard at her grandpa. 'You just said that a traveller needed our help and told me to send out a selection of our mechanimals to assist them.'

'Oh, I thought you knew,' said a very contrite Jakeman. Then he brightened up. 'But the good news is that the factory clock, which hadn't worked for years, now keeps perfect time!' he said.

'I'm sure Charlie's thrilled about that!' cried Philly.

'There's no point playing the blame game,' interrupted Theo. 'How *are* we going to send Charlie back to where he belongs?'

'And don't even suggest that thing again,' I said, pointing at the cannon. Then I had an idea. 'I've already made it back once,' I said. 'I went along a tunnel that led all the way from the Forest of Skulls to my back garden. How did that happen? It closed up behind me, but perhaps I could find another tunnel.'

'That was just pure chance, Charlie. There are bound to be faults in the fabric of time and space; little worm holes that lead between the worlds,' said Jakeman. 'But the chances of us finding another tunnel that leads to your world, in your time, must be a trillion to one at least.'

'Oh, brilliant,' I cried. 'Now I'll never be able to get home.'

'Wait a minute – everyone calm down,' said Philly. 'I think I might have a solution. Do you still have the data from your original experiment, Grandpa?'

A Marvellous Map

With an armful of printouts, Philly sat down at one of the computers that were lined up along a workbench and began tapping at the keyboard.

'If we feed all this data in, we should be able to pinpoint exactly where the hole between our worlds was made,' said Philly. 'We have angle of laser, direction and speed of beam, and parameters of error.'

Her fingers tapped busily.

'Yeah, but what . . .' began Jakeman.

'Shush,' said Philly. 'I'm concentrating.'

'Oh, very sorry I'm sure,' said Jakeman looking rather hurt.

'What does that say, Grandpa?' asked Philly a little less snappily. 'Two fisbates – what's a fisbate?'

'No, two fishcakes,' said Jakeman. 'I was writing down what to have for tea.'

With a tut, Philly deleted the entry from the computer and carried on typing, her fingers just a blur. 'Now, if I convert this data into a graphic representation and overlay it on a map of our world, it should show us . . .' She pressed ENTER and we watched as a thin red line began to creep a winding path across a map of the surrounding landscape.

'Yep, it's working. Look!' she cried. The line started at the factory and travelled across seas, over moors and through a great city before finally stopping at a bend in a wide river, where it started to flash.

'There you are, Charlie,' said Philly, pressing more keys. A printer started to whirr and a second later she handed me an amazing map.

'Brilliant!' I said. 'Is this what I think it is?'

'Sure is. That's where your destiny lies, Charlie; that's where you've got to go,' Philly said, smiling and pointing to where the line met the river.

(see next page)

'Fantastic!' I exclaimed, still not quite able to believe it. 'You mean that if I go to this place I will pass through a tear in space and time, back into my own world?'

'Yep!'

'Are you sure?'

'Sure I'm sure,' she said.

'Wow!' I gasped, my hands starting to shake a little. I was holding the most important document of my life – a passport home.

'Just make sure you don't lose it, Charlie,' she

said. 'Or you really will be up a creek without a paddle.'

'Smart thinking, Philly,' said Jakeman. 'One day you will be as great a scientist as me.'

'One day?' said Philly with a grin.

'There's only one problem,' I said. 'How am I going to get there?'

'Just carry on walking, of course,' said Philly. 'At least you know where you're going now.'

'It's a mighty long way,' I said. I was starting to have second thoughts. The more I studied the map, the more dangerous the journey appeared. 'And look at the places I have to travel through: The Sea of Lost Souls; Darkmoor; The Mountains of the Jagged Edge. They don't sound very friendly.'

'Well if you're going to pick holes in my plan, just for the sake of it,' said Philly, becoming sulky again.

'Don't worry, Charlie,' said Jakeman. 'I might have just the thing to help you on your way.' He hurried across the factory floor and disappeared through a large door marked INVENTIONS PENDING.

We waited as a series of crashes and bangs came from inside. Then, 'Aha!' we heard the old inventor cry. 'Here it is.' And the next minute he reappeared carrying the most incredible-looking machine. 'Here you are, Charlie. Your very own Air-rider!'

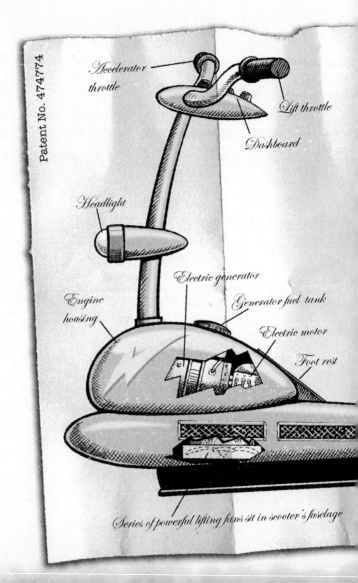

Patent No. 474774

Accelerator throttle

Lift throttle

Dashboard

Headlight

Electric generator

Generator fuel tank

Electric motor

Engine housing

Foot rest

Series of powerful lifting fans sit in scooter's fuselage

The Air-rider

This is the fantabulous machine that Jakeman got from his storeroom:

Jakeman's Incredible

Air-rider

- Goes like a rocket!
- Goes on for ever!
- Amaze your friends!
- Learn to hover, flip and spin!
- This is not a toy!

Mechanical Marvels For All Occasions!

Stabilizing fin

Drive fan

Footplate

Air intake vents for lifting fans

Air skirt

It's a scooter without any wheels and looks super-cool. It floats on a cushion of air sucked in by small, powerful fans through side vents and directed downwards to where it is trapped by a rubber skirt around the base – just like a hovercraft. A handle-bar accelerator grip is wired to a larger fan on the back to propel the machine forwards.

'Oh, wicked,' I said, running my hands over the sleek paintwork. Now I could hardly wait to get going. 'How fast will it go?'

'About sixty-five kilometres an hour,' said Jakeman. 'And if you take it steady, you should be able to ride it on water as well as land. Perhaps you'd like to try it out in the yard.'

We all trooped outside into the sunshine and Jakeman placed the scooter on the ground. I stepped onto the footplate.

'Now, press the starter button on the console,' said Jakeman.

Wooooom! The interior fans started up and the machine lifted from the ground.

'Left throttle for lift, right throttle to go forwards,' said Jakeman. 'That's all you need to know!'

I twisted the left throttle all the way and the

scooter rose about a metre from the ground.

'Whoa!' I cried as the machine wobbled and
I nearly tumbled off. I decreased the power and
dropped down; at the same time I twisted the
right grip. The back fan began to spin and the
Air-rider moved smoothly forward.

'It's brilliant,' I said. I was very wobbly at first.
It was like trying to learn how to ride a bike all
over again, but this time you had to think about
lift as well as speed and balance. Soon, though, I
got the hang of it and zoomed round the yard.
I went into a tight turn and pulled up next to
Jakeman.

'Everything OK?' he asked, handing me my
rucksack.

'Perfect,' I said – and then I suddenly felt sad,
because I realized the time had come for me
to leave. I pulled on my explorer's kit. 'Well, I
s'pose I'd better be on my way,' I added lamely.

Jakeman put his hand on my shoulder. 'Take
care, Charlie Small, and good luck. You're the
bravest explorer in the history of any world
and it's been great to meet you. Sorry about the
cannon and all that.'

I gave the old inventor a hug round his fat
tummy. He and his many inventions had looked

after me through all my adventures and I would never forget him.

I said a fond farewell to Theo and Harmonia, and then turned to say cheerio to Philly herself.

'Bye, Charlie,' she said, looking at the ground.

'Bye,' I replied, awkwardly putting out my hand to shake. There was a bit of a silence, then Philly suddenly rushed forwards, planted a kiss on my cheek and ran back inside Jakeman's Factory.

I started up the Air-rider again, feeling very embarrassed. 'What about fuel?' I asked the inventor.

'Don't worry about that, Charlie,' said my old friend. 'I've filled it with my own petrol concentrate. There's enough fuel in the tank to go twice round the world!'

'Thanks,' I said, then revved the throttle and with a final wave shot through the gates and away.

'I'll be following your progress on my radar,' cried Jakeman. 'Good luck, Charlie.'

Off To The Seaside!

I whizzed across the high cliff tops where the factory stood, waves crashing noisily below me. I followed the route marked on the map as closely as possible; around headlands, over ditches, through the winding streets of a little port, and I'd soon left the factory far behind.

I was feeling a bit empty inside after saying a final farewell to my friends, but as the orange sun began to set below the horizon and a clear, warm night lay before me, I began to enjoy myself once more. The scooter was easy to control and it wasn't long before I was trying out some tricks, just like the ones I did on my bike at home – 180 G turns; bunnyhops and a new one, only possible on an Air-rider – the vertical launch and spin. *Yeehah*, it was brilliant!

By the time the pale moon was high in the sky, I'd arrived at a sandy beach dotted with large rocks and I decided to make camp. I lay my very old and tatty coat on the sand in the shelter of a rock shaped like a lumpy loaf of bread, and stretched out. I was tired – driving the Airrider all afternoon and half the night had made my arms and legs ache. I was feeling mighty hungry too and opened my rucksack. Oh good, someone had filled my water bottle right up and made a large packet of doorstep sandwiches for me too. I bet it was Philly; it's just the thoughtful sort of thing she'd do.

I glugged down some water and ripped open the sandwich bag. They were my favourite – tomato sauce and crushed-crisp sarnies. Not very healthy, but delicious! I finished off half the sandwiches, had another glug of water and then tipped the contents out of my rucksack. It was about time I checked my explorer's kit.

Oh, fantastic! Not only did I have all my usual things, but Jakeman had added a few extra items of his own invention. My kit now contained:

1) My multi-tooled penknife
2) A brand new ball of string (extra strong)*
3) A nearly full water bottle and four energy bars*
4) A telescope
5) A scarf (complete with bullet holes!)

6) An old railway ticket (I've forgotten where this came from)

7) My journal

8) A pack of wild animal collector's cards (full of amazing animal facts)

9) A brand new glue pen to stick things in my notebook*

10) A glass eye from my brave steam-powered rhinoceros friend

11) The compass and torch I found on the sun-bleached skeleton of a lost explorer

12) The tooth of a monstrous megashark (makes a handy saw)

13) A magnifying glass (for starting fires etc.)

14) A radio

15) My mobile phone with wind-up charger (to speak to Mum)

16) The (broken) skull of a Barbarous Bat

17) A bundle of maps and diagrams collected on my adventures

18) A bag of marbles

19) Four brand new, shiny metal balls labelled, 'SMOKE BOMBS'*

One of the shiny metal smoke bombs

20) The bony finger of an animated skeleton (handy for picking locks)
21) A fantastic wristband that could shoot out a small, metal anchor on a long string (this could be really useful for climbing and swinging)*

* New or replenished items

Before putting the stuff back in my bag, I decided it would be a good time to phone Mum and let her know I was finally on my way home. Not that she would understand me – she is stuck at the time I started these brilliant adventures and always says the same thing, no matter what I tell her! Still, it's good to hear her voice. I charged my mobile and dialled the number.

'Hi, Mum,' I said when she answered.

'Charlie, is that you? Is everything all right?'

'Yes, Mum, everything's fine – I'm finally on my way home,' I replied. 'I've just got to cross a wild ocean, a bleak moorland and a few other obstacles before I get there. It's going to be really dangerous.'

'Sounds wonderful, dear,' said Mum.

'I'm travelling on a floating scooter called an Air-rider,' I continued. 'A crazy old inventor built it for me and it goes like a rocket!'

'Ooh, that's nice,' said Mum cheerily. 'Wait a minute, Charlie. Here's your dad just come in. Now remember, don't be late for tea.'

'See you soon, Mum,' I said and she hung up.

Now I've finished writing up these notes, I'm going to get some kip. In the morning I'll have to set out across the Sea of Lost Souls. It doesn't sound like a very cheery place, and from the size of it on the map, it'll take me more than one day to reach my destination. I hope I don't go to sleep and fall off the Air-rider!

I'll write more just as soon as I can.

The Sea Of Lost Souls

The next morning I finished off my sandwiches, splashed my face in the sea, then started up the Air-rider and steered to the water's edge.

I held my breath as I left the beach, not knowing how the scooter would handle on the sea, but the water was as calm as a millpond and, apart from a slight wobble, there were no problems. I opened up the throttle, gunned the motor and went scudding along at top speed. The sun was out, there was a fresh wind and the silver sea looked as if it were made of mercury.

The Sea of Lost Souls doesn't seem a very accurate name for this place, I thought. *It's beautiful.*

Two hours later, though, I was starting to get bored. I hadn't even spotted a seagull. The sea was vast and flat and empty; there wasn't so much as a piece of flotsam floating by.

Four hours later I was going crazy with boredom, and the bright sun on the water was making my eyes and head ache.

'Please, something happen!' I yelled. Even a fish's fin breaking the surface would be a treat, but my voice seemed lost in the vast space and the water stayed as smooth as glass.

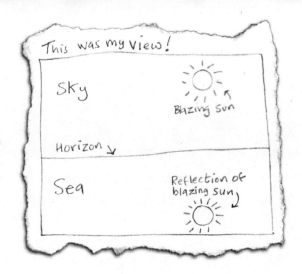

This was my view!

Sky

Blazing Sun

Horizon ↓

Sea

Reflection of blazing sun

After what seemed an eternity, the sun began to set and I turned on the scooter's headlight. Now I had the problem of what to do for the night. My head was pounding from sunstroke, my arms were aching and I didn't fancy trying to balance on the scooter all night. It didn't look as if I would have any choice, though – there wasn't so much as a rocky outcrop on which to spend the night.

Then, at last, I spotted something in the fading light – a small, dark shape was bobbing about on the water. As I got closer, I realized it was a rowing boat floating aimlessly on the sluggish water. *It must have broken free from its mooring and drifted out to sea,* I thought. *And lucky for me it did!*

I pulled up alongside. There was nothing in the tiny dinghy but a rumpled tarpaulin, so I shut down the Air-rider and stepped aboard. I pulled the scooter in after me and collapsed in the bottom of the boat, thoroughly exhausted.

'Ouch!' I said as something sharp dug in my side. 'What the heck is that?' I flipped back the tarpaulin and . . .

'Oh my goodness!' I cried, for sharing the boat with me was a horrible human skeleton, the hollow eyes of its chalky-white skull staring back at me and its toothy jaw set in a terrible grin.

The skeleton was wearing ragged clothes, partly rotted by the salty air; a three-cornered hat sat on top of its head and a tangle of long, curly hair sprouted from below its brim. A wide leather belt hung loose around the skeleton's bony hips, with a scabbard holding a long, curved scimitar. It was one of the most gruesome sights I'd ever seen. Even worse – I was sure I recognized the clothes and sword. This skinny seafarer was none other than Sabre Sue, the pirate who had taught me how to swordfight.

Noticing a scrap of paper protruding from

(See my journal Pirate Galleon)

The ghastly remains of Sabre Sue Yuk!

her coat pocket, I pulled it out. On one side was a black spot, the pirate's sentence of death; on the other a message that I read with mounting horror.

A Warning To All Pirates

This buccaneer was set adrift as punishment for disobeying the orders of her Captain. Also for being a snitch and too girly to be a proper pirate. Let it stand as a lesson to all brigands of the briny. Do as you're told or suffer the consequences.

Signed, *Cut-throat*

Captain and Scourge of the High Seas

So, Captain Cut-throat was still up to her old tricks. I really hope I don't bump into her again. The last time we met, we didn't part on the friendliest of terms!

I didn't want to spend the night with a rotting skeleton, so I decided to give her a proper pirate's funeral. After unclipping the sword (I couldn't pass up the opportunity to arm myself with such a formidable weapon) I wrapped the body in the tarpaulin, tied it with some rope I found in the boat and rolled her over the side.

As the skeleton sank beneath the torpid sea, I recited a Pirate's Prayer:

Go down to Davy Jones' locker,
And rest on the bed of the sea,
Where fish flash like silver and gold,
And all of the grog is free.
Shiver me timbers, Amen!

Then, with a heavy heart and the stars twinkling in a vast and clear sky above me, I fell into a deep sleep, my dreams populated by a horde of pirates all trying to hand me the black spot!

I slept like a log, and when I woke up this morning the sun was already high in the sky. I have eaten one of the energy bars in my rucksack and taken a good swig of water. I have to be very careful with my supplies, as I don't know when I'll be able to stock up again.

I'm just finishing writing these notes and then I'll be on my way. The sea is still as calm as a pond, the horizon still empty and the sun still as hot as a frying pan. Looks like I've got another long day ahead of me. I've decided to tow the dinghy along behind me, just in case I need it for another night. I'll write more soon.

Land Ahoy!

Oh boy, what a very scary voyage! I'm safe now, but at one point I thought I'd never make it to dry land.

As soon as I'd finished writing my journal, I hopped onto the Air-rider, tied the dinghy to the back and went zooming across the Sea of Lost Souls. My Air-rider was brilliant — its little fans kept on whirring for mile after mile. I spent another night aboard the dinghy; but when I woke up on that third morning, things had started to change.

Great grey clouds were rolling across the sky and a stiff breeze was disturbing the surface of the sea. An hour later the breeze had grown into a hurricane and the sea was a frenzy of mountainous waves. I hung on to the handlebars for dear life as I was sent racing to the top of towering, watery peaks and then sucked down into the dark, roaring valleys between them.

The storm raged for hours and the fans on my scooter were no match for the terrible forces of nature that picked me up and dropped me down as if I were a toy. The dinghy broke loose and was washed away. I was buffeted, battered and soaked to my goose-pimpled skin.

All I could do was hold on and close my eyes to keep out the terrifying sight of monstrous, watery caves opening in the sea before me. They swallowed me whole, whisked me round as if I were in a spin dryer, then spat me out again.

Up and down and round and round I went, as if on a never-ending fairground ride. My ears were ringing with the screaming wind and my skin stung as I was whipped with sea spray. Then, as if by magic, the black clouds above me parted like great billowing curtains; a shaft of sunlight shone down and the storm died. It was as if someone had pulled the plug from a giant wind machine.

Breathing heavily, my heart pounding and my limbs as weak as water, I opened my salt-crusted eyes and looked around. The sea rolled slowly, as if it were as thick as cream, still stretching out before me as far as I could see. *Oh no,* I thought. *After all that I'm still in the middle of nowhere!* Then the squawk of a seagull made me turn round, and there, a hundred metres away, was the long arm of a sandy bay.

'Yeehah!' I cried, spinning the Air-rider round and driving up onto the scrubby sand dunes that lined the beach. At last I was on solid ground.

I collapsed onto the sand and didn't move for an hour. Finally I sat up and took such a long swig from my water bottle, I nearly drained it dry. My arms ached like billy-o, but there were still a few hours of daylight left and I knew I should get on with my journey and find some fresh water.

I checked the GPS system on the handlebar dashboard of the Air-rider. To my surprise, the storm hadn't blown me far off course, so I started up the softly humming fans and set off over the rolling dunes.

A Suffocating Swarm

I hadn't gone far when I saw a dark, shifting cloud ahead and thought I was in for another storm. As I got closer though, I realized it was only a few metres from the ground. *What the heck is it?* I wondered. *Whoa!* All of a sudden the cloud engulfed me and a million, miniscule insects no bigger than pinheads swarmed around my head.

They went up my nose, in my eyes and into my mouth making it hard to breathe. I coughed and spluttered, tumbling from my scooter as I spat out a paste of squashed midges. I was being suffocated by the manky microdots! It was like breathing solid air and I fell to my knees, gasping. I frantically felt inside my explorer's kit and my hand closed around one of Jakeman's metallic smoke bombs.

I threw it down, but the sandy ground was soft and the bomb didn't break, so I snatched it up and cracked it against the scooter. The ball split open and a thick plume of smoke poured out like an erupting volcano. The midges immediately scattered, but now I couldn't

My head was lost in a cloud of pests the size of pinheads!

breathe because of the smoke! I dropped to the ground where the air was clearer and gulped in huge lungfuls of precious oxygen.

As the smoke dispersed, I picked up the Air-rider and gunned the engine, scooting away before the cloud of midges came back. The sand dunes went on for miles, like a rolling golden desert, but I eventually scooted to the top of the very last hill and saw an enormous moorland spreading out before me. I checked the map – I was about to enter a wild, windswept wasteland called Darkmoor.

I could see where it got its name – the lonely landscape was folded into ridges and dips like a rumpled old brown and green carpet. There were pools of water as dark as gravy in the shadow of big, grey rocks and a line of thin trees, bent over like a queue of doddery grannies, ran along the horizon. The wide, grey sky looked threatening and full of rain.

'Oh, what a lovely place, I *don't* think,' I muttered. But I knew I would have to make camp soon, so I scooted down from the dunes and, as I motored across the springy moor grasses, looked for somewhere safe to sleep.

Making Camp

I found a sheltered spot in a grassy hollow and, where the ground sloped steeply up a bank, I took the megashark's tooth from my explorer's kit and started to cut three sides of a large rectangle in the soft turf. With this done I then forced the tooth flat under the grass and began to loosen it from the soil below so I could roll it back like a thick blanket.

The next thing was to find some strong supports, and with Sabre Sue's scimitar I hacked off two straight branches from one of the windswept trees. These I pushed into the ground and then, taking the two corners of the fold of grass, hooked them over the stakes, making a thick grassy roof.

My shelter

This would protect me from the fine rain that was starting to fall again, and the slope at the back would protect me from the worst of the wind.

Taking the sword I went scavenging for food, always keeping my stripy scarf in view, which I'd tied to the support of my shelter to act as a beacon. It was easy to spot in the dull, olive green landscape of the moor. I found a small stream of clear water and filled my water bottle to the brim. I didn't have any luck grub-hunting though, and I've had to eat another of my energy bars. I'm getting worryingly low on food, so tomorrow I'll have to step up my search.

The air has turned very chilly now the sun has set, but the soft earth remains warm and I'm quite snug in my little hollow. I've been studying the map by torchlight – what a long, long way I have to travel before I reach the spot where I can pass back into my own world! It's even further than I thought.

The wind is howling like a lost spirit, the branches of the trees are rattling like a ghost's chains and a mist is starting to form on the ground like a swirling phantom. Oh, jeepers! Goodnight – I'll write more soon.

Spectral Shapes

When I woke up the following morning, the moor was swathed in a thick, swirling mist that muffled the sounds of the dawn birds and made everything seem seriously spooky. I broke camp and carefully rode the Air-rider through the vapour, jumping as great boulders loomed suddenly out of the murk like huge hunched ghosts.

I drove at a crawling pace with my nerves all a-jangle, expecting some sort of slavering spectre to appear at any moment – but nothing happened. My trusty machine whirred away, suspending me above the dew-soaked grass for hour after hour. I heard the growls and yelps of animals and peered blindly into the fog for a glimpse of them, but they remained hidden in the shifting banks of cloud.

As a beam of golden sunlight suddenly penetrated the mist and started to break it up into wispy, raggedy tendrils, I got the shock of my life. I saw someone coming towards me through the thinning fog. I slowed down – and he slowed as well. Uh-oh, I didn't like this one little bit. The figure seemed to fade and then reappear as the mist shifted. I edged forward and so did the stranger. All of a sudden I could see him quite clearly. It was a ghostly, scruffy boy riding a scooter with a heavy rucksack on his back.

'Bloomin' heck,' I whispered. 'It's me!' I was meeting myself coming the other way!

Then as the sun grew stronger and the fog melted away, so did my hazy twin and with a rush of relief, I realized what had happened. By a crazy trick of the light, I had seen my image reflected from the wall of vapour.

'That was weird,' I said to myself, my heart still pounding away. Now though, with the sun up and the mist gone, everything looked safe and normal again. In fact, Darkmoor looked as fresh as a new painting. The grass was a thousand soft shades of ochre and green and sparkled with dew. The sky was a huge arc of clear blue and larks, plovers and curlews sang and peeped merrily.

'See,' I reassured myself, opening the throttle on the scooter and buzzing along at top speed. 'There's absolutely nothing to be frightened of.' Oh boy, won't I ever learn?

On a ridge of high ground ahead, I could see a cluster of Tors – tall towers of odd-shaped boulders that looked as if a giant baby had been stacking pebbles. My route took me right past them and, as I eased on the accelerator to have a look at the strange structures, I saw some fat mushrooms growing around the base of one. My tummy rumbled. 'Aha! Breakfast, I believe!'

I said, stepping off the scooter.

I strode through the long tufts of damp grass on a series of stepping-stones, as big and flat as paving slabs, which led to the base of the towering Tor. Crouching down to inspect the fungi, I tried to remember everything my sprite pal, Spriggot, had taught me about identifying mushrooms. I know some of them are deadly poisonous, but I recognized these immediately and knew they would be quite safe to eat, so I picked an armful, rubbed away the crumbly, soft soil and bit into one.

Mini Monsters And Bubbling Bogs

It was delicious – meaty and peppery – and I soon scoffed down two or three and stuffed the others into my rucksack for later. As I turned to go, one of the stepping-stones slowly rose up as if on a hinge. Underneath was a wet, muddy chamber, and something was moving around inside.

With a horrified gasp I stepped back as a thing the size and shape of a football leaped out from its hole, growling like a menacing mastiff. An overpowering stench of rotting vegetables hit me, making my tummy turn over in disgust. One by one the other slabs lifted up and more cannonball-shaped creatures sprang out, forming a half-circle in front of me. They didn't seem very friendly!

Their damp, shiny skin was bluish-grey and they had glowering eyes as yellow as lemons. Their spherical bodies were really just big slobbering mouths with teeth like pebbles set in purple, warty gums, and their fetid breath stank to high heaven. The creatures sat on very short legs with wide webbed feet, and swung themselves around on long muscular arms.

'Good things; nice little moorland monsters,' I said, holding my nose and backing away as they slowly edged forwards, growling as if they had little motors in their throats, and gnashing their teeth. 'Stay, there's good whatchamacallits.'

But they didn't stay; they advanced towards

One of the
gurgling
gristle-balls
Yikes!

me. One of the creatures picked up a large
stone, hefted it in his hand and then lobbed it. It
hit me on the shoulder with a whack.

'Yeow! Clear off, you gristle-balls,' I shouted,
rubbing my arm and kicking some gravelly
dirt towards them. It was the wrong reaction,

because now all twelve of the football-shaped fiends picked up pebbles and sharp nuggets of flint and threw them. I turned and crouched, the stones painfully bouncing off my back. Then, covering my head with my arms and still crouching low, I ran as fast as I could towards my scooter. I bent down to get it, but another hail of stones hit me and I knew if I stopped for even a second I would be overwhelmed. I scuttled down the slope with the yowling, yelping things hot on my heels.

At the bottom of the slope was a flat area of vivid green grass and I careered across it like an Olympic sprinter. It was very wet and the legs of my jeans were soon soaked through. Then I noticed my pursuers had stopped. They were standing at the edge of the dark green area, a couple of hundred metres away, gurgling like noisy drains. I slowed down, looking back over my shoulder at the critters; they weren't even throwing stones any more. Perhaps they were scared of water.

'Good riddance!' I yelled, but when I tried to run again I found it was impossible. My feet weighed a ton and I couldn't lift them from the ground. *What the heck?* I thought, and looked down to find my feet weren't there – neither were my knees! I was in a quagmire and I was slowly but surely sinking.

I tried to pull my legs from the sucking, gluey mud but I couldn't budge an inch. I was stuck and I was in big, big trouble.

My feet weren't there!

'Help me, you useless bags of wind,' I bellowed at the growling globes, but they just gurgled with merriment and chucked a few stones at me for target practise. 'No, come back!' I yelled as they became bored and started to leave, planting their long arms on the ground and then swinging their bodies through them to land on their webbed feet like strange spherical chimps. They didn't give me a backward glance.

'Help, someone help me!' I cried at the top of my voice. I was now up to my waist in mud as thick as cold porridge. The moor monsters had gone and I was completely on my own. What could I do?

I quickly took off my rucksack and scrabbled around inside – there was nothing there to help me. I was doomed! Then I remembered the wristband that Jakeman had added to my kit. I'd already strapped it around my wrist and now was the perfect time to try it out. I looked around but the only thing in range was a hunched, lone tree

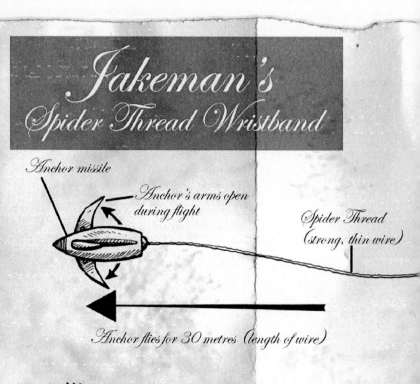

Jakeman's
Spider Thread Wristband

Anchor missile

Anchor's arms open during flight

Spider Thread (strong, thin wire)

Anchor flies for 30 metres (length of wire)

Patent No. 474775

growing on a hump in the middle of the bright green bog. As I sank even lower and the mud squidged under my armpits, I pointed my wrist towards the tree and pressed the firing button on the band with my other hand.

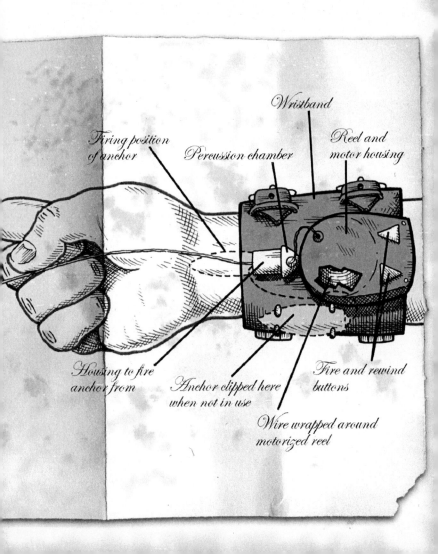

Wristband

Firing position of anchor

Percussion chamber

Reel and motor housing

Housing to fire anchor from

Anchor clipped here when not in use

Wire wrapped around motorized reel

Fire and rewind buttons

Thok! The silver anchor-shaped missile shot as fast as a bullet from its mounting, trailing a thin wire behind it. It arced over the bog and rattled to a halt among the twisted branches of the tree. I pressed another button that started a little motor and the wristband began to reel the wire back in. The anchor caught hold of one of the branches and, as the motor whirred and the wire shortened, my body was gradually pulled from the clinging mud like a cork from a bottle.

It felt like I was being stretched on a rack as, with loud *gloops*, first my waist, then my legs and finally my feet were hauled from the stinking mire and I was towed across the top of the bog. Eventually I was able to grab the base of the tree and climb up onto the small mound of solid ground. Exhausted, I flopped down and looked around me. I was safe – safe, but marooned on a tiny island in the middle of a deadly quagmire. Now, how the heck was I going to get off?

Howling For Help

I thought and thought, studying my explorer's kit again – but without something to shoot the anchor missile at, there was no way to get off the mound. So I did the only thing I could think of – I hollered for help!

'Heeeelp! Heeeeeelp!' I yelled and yelled until my throat ached, my voice carrying clearly over the empty moor. I stopped and listened. Nothing. I hollered again – and again – and again. 'Heeeeeelp!' – and then, in the distance, I heard a reply.

'Waaoow!'

'Help me. I'm stuck on an island in the middle of a bog!' I shouted.

'Waaoow!' came the reply again. Then I realized it wasn't the call of a person, but the howl of an animal; and it was a cry I thought I recognized. Surely it couldn't be!

'Waaoow!' I howled back, hardly daring to hope; but as the animal's reply grew closer and closer, I was sure. Through the spiky grass he came, barking in excitement – the wonderful white wolf I had befriended in my fight against the terrible Puppet Master.

(See my journal The Puppet Master's Prison)

'Braemar! It *is* you,' I called. 'No, stop, it's not safe!' I added as he went to rush headlong into the quagmire. The wolf pulled up just in time and looked quizzically at me. 'Just wait there, boy.' I extended my arm like an archer and hit the fire button on the wristband. *Whoosh!* The missile flew over the quagmire and landed next to Braemar.

Through the spiky grass he came

'Grab it, Braemar, and hold on tight,' I cried and the clever wolf clamped his powerful jaws around the wire. I immediately started the motor to reel the wire back in and once again I was dragged across the surface of the bog until Braemar was able to grab my collar and drag me up to safety on the bank of dry ground.

'Phewee! Braemar, you're a life-saver,' I said. Instantly the great white wolf dived on me and began licking my face in delight. 'OK,' I chuckled, pushing the huge animal off. 'I'm wet enough already, thanks. Let's get out of here while we have the chance.'

Getting to my feet, I cautiously retraced my steps to where I'd left my scooter, checking around for any sign of the horrible creatures that had driven me into the mire. I couldn't see any, but as we approached the Tor, a couple of the rock slabs lifted a fraction and I saw a flash of lemon-coloured eyes and caught a whiff of decomposing vegetation.

One of the creatures crept right out, then caught sight of Braemar and with a squeal darted back to its hole. The wolf leaped, but the globe of gristle was too quick. Braemar sniffed and growled and scraped around the slab in frustration but, thank goodness, the cretinous critter was too scared to come back out.

'Let's get out of here,' I said to the wolf, starting up the Air-rider, and with the beautiful beast bounding beside me I zoomed away, past the quagmire and across Darkmoor, following the route marked on my precious map.

Once we had covered a good distance and I knew we'd be safe, I pulled up and sat down for a rest and a spot of lunch. I broke up the remainder of my mushrooms and shared them with my brave friend.

'Thanks for coming to the rescue, Braemar,' I said, stroking his big, furry white mane.

The wolf barked in answer as he suspiciously sniffed at the fungi. Then, making up his mind, he scoffed his pile down in one. As we ate, I opened my Wild Animal Collector's Cards and shuffled through them to see if they had any info on my attackers. Sure enough, there was a card and here is what it said.

Looks like I got off lightly, I thought, returning the cards to my explorer's kit. As I finished my mushrooms, I looked at the wonderful wolf, sitting patiently

PREDATOR RATING 6

The Wartbog

Wartbogs are ferocious fiends that live near moorland mires. Their bodies are nearly all stomach, leaving little room for a brain. They drive trespassers to a muddy end in the nearest bilious bog. Eating only rotting vegetation their smelly breaths could stun a large horse. Few people survive a Wartbog attack.

WILD ANIMAL COLLECTORS CARDS

and watching me with alert, intelligent eyes.

'It's so good to see you, Braemar. I wonder what you've been up to since we last met. It'd be great if you could come along with me. I could do with some company. Look, this is where I'm heading,' I said, unfolding the map and laying it on the tufty grass. Braemar sniffed at the map and gave another small bark, then looked over his shoulder, across the moor.

'What is it, boy – have you got to go?' I asked. He whined at me, poring the ground and nuzzling my neck.

On the wind I heard a call. 'Waaoow!'

Braemar immediately lifted his head and howled in response. A minute later, I saw a she-wolf and four cubs standing on a rise, silhouetted against the bright afternoon sky.

'Oh wow, is that your family?' I asked.

'Woof,' replied the wolf as the cubs started to yap and play-fight around their mother.

'Well, you'd better go and look after them,' I said, wrapping my arms around his neck and burying my face deep in his fur. The wolf gave me one last lick, then bounded up the slope to join his wife and cubs.

'Thanks, Braemar,' I called. 'Waaooow!'

'Waaoow!' the whole family called back and then, in a flash, were gone.

Feeling a little empty and alone, I got back on the scooter and carried on with my journey.

A Place For The Night

Now I was heading into the very heart of Darkmoor, an area even more windswept and threatening than before. Great dark pools of brackish water lay on the surface of the moor; birds of prey screeched high above; dense gorse bushes with thorns as long as your fingers grew in impenetrable clumps; and herds of wild ponies stood motionless and forlorn, heads lowered against the chill wind.

I drove my scooter through the afternoon and into the evening, fighting the buffeting wind and getting soaked by a fine drizzle. The ground was too open to make a camp for the night, so I steered the Air-rider away from my route and headed towards a high crest of ground on the horizon. Great lumps of granite broke through the turf and would offer some shelter from the weather.

As I settled down in a small, natural alcove in one of the granite blocks, I heard an indistinct cry on the wind and my heart missed a beat. It was definitely a man calling – but would he be a friend or a foe? I crept from my hidey-hole and peered over the rocks to the far side of the ridge.

The moorland beyond was as flat as a pancake. The blurred silhouette of a copse of trees stood in the middle-distance and the land in front was criss-crossed with drainage ditches and dikes. In the patchwork fields between the ditches, I could make out a handful of tall, very thin men stooping over in the rain, up to their ankles in mud, digging at the soil and lifting crops. They moved very slowly as if they were exhausted from their toil.

Well, they look harmless enough, I thought. *Should I go and say hello?* I wasn't sure, so decided to leave my scooter and sword amongst the rocks and creep down to get a closer look. I crawled on my belly over the damp grass, feeling very exposed on the flat, featureless plain, until I could duck down into one of the ditches. Yuck! The muddy water came up to my knees, but at least I was out of sight and could wade up one ditch and down another until I was much closer to the workers.

I peeped over the top of the bank. One of the men was just a couple of metres away, and a very odd-looking chap he was! He was wearing a battered grey hat above a face so long and narrow it looked as if he'd been passed through a mangle. He had sad, dark eyes with great, green-tinged bags underneath, and the lobes of his ears flapped down almost to his shoulder.

He moved slowly, as did all the workers, pulling at the beet with long, spatula-shaped fingers and dropping them into a sack slung over his shoulders. I was trying to decide whether to make myself known, when a strident voice with a strong Texan twang broke the silence, and I ducked back down. Then I heard footsteps squelching over the soggy field.

'Hurry up, you spoon-fingered dolt, the sun's going down and we're wanting our dinner,' the voice said.

I parted some rushes and peered out again, just in time to see a large man boot the poor worker on the backside, knocking him onto his knees in the mud. The crop-picker didn't say a word, but just got slowly to his feet and carried on working.

'That's enough, take your bags to the kitchens and then get your carcasses back to your huts,' the man shouted. He was tall and rather fat with a fancy waistcoat stretched over his barrel-shaped belly; his small eyes peered from the fleshy folds of his wide, flat face and, as I stared more closely at him through the driving drizzle, I got the shock of my life. I knew him!

As the workers began walking slowly away, I heard another voice approaching. As he came into view I received another shock. I knew this guy as well! This one was immensely fat with a big wedge of a nose and a bald head covered in a pattern of black tattoos.

I couldn't believe it – standing before me were two of my enemies from previous adventures: Horatio Ham, mayor of Trouble Town in the Wild West, and Belcher, the Brigand chief of Frostbite Pass; a pair of the biggest crooks imaginable! What were they

(see my Journal Frostbite Pass)

doing together? What the heck were they doing in the middle of a dark and lonely moor? Then I heard a click behind me. It was the sound of a pistol being cocked.

'Oh dearie me, if it isn't Charlie Small, don't you know,' said a very familiar sing-song voice. 'What are you skulking around in that dirty ditch for? Come out at once!' I turned round to find Tristram Twitch, the dandified criminal cretin I'd met in my adventure at the Mummy's Tomb, holding a fringed umbrella in one hand and waving a tiny, ivory-handled pistol at me with the other.

'Charlie Small?' cried Horatio Ham in his nasal twang, spinning round. 'I hoped I'd seen the last of you!'

'Likewise, I'm sure,' I muttered under my breath.

'Charlie Small!' growled Belcher in a rich, fruity voice. ''Ow did you get 'ere, you pernicious pest?'

Feeling that all my worst nightmares had come true at the same time, I hauled myself from the ditch and stood before my old enemies.

'Spying on us again are you, you 'orrible

(See my journal The Mummy's Tomb)

Belcher

Twitch

Ham

'ooligan?' asked Belcher, cracking the knuckles of his big, fat hands.

'Yeah, you've got a nerve, after everything you did to me,' said Ham, his small, piggy eyes almost lost in the ruddy folds of his chubby cheeks.

'Look, I'm not spying on you. I just happen to be passing through on my way home,' I said, trying to appear nonchalant. 'So, if you don't mind, I'll say cheerio and be on my way.' I turned to walk away, but I hadn't taken two paces before a hand on my collar stopped me in my tracks.

'Oh, I don't think so, Charlie,' said Belcher with a chuckle, his thick voice sounding like he had a permanent cold. 'We can't leave you out here on a filthy night like this, dear boy. You must come back with us.'

'Na, you're all right. I'm quite happy out here,' I said, trying to break away again.

'Hold on there, you son-of-a-gun,' drawled Ham. 'Belcher's right, we'll put you up.'

'Indubitably, Charlie,' sniggered Twitch. 'I'd never forgive myself if you caught a chill.'

I was marched before my captors across the muddy fields. All the workers had disappeared by now and the light in the sky was fading fast. Tristram Twitch pranced across the mud like a pony, umbrella held high, desperately trying to keep his fancy clothes clean.

'Oh, typical,' he cried in anguish. 'That's another pair of silk hose absolutely ruined.'

We crossed one ditch after another by way of small, plank bridges and eventually came to a wide gravel drive that led through the centre of the cultivated area towards the copse of trees. As the rain-sodden sky grew darker, I began to make out some twinkling lights between the leaves and I assumed we were heading towards the crooks' campfire.

I started to shiver with cold as we crunched along the path in silence, passing under an arched tunnel of dripping branches that led through the trees and out the other side. In front of us, lights glowing brightly in the windows, stood the dark shape of a big, fine house.

Another Shock!

The drive crossed a dirty moat over a low, rickety bridge and we walked into a cobbled courtyard through a pair of wrought-iron gates. Low stable blocks lined two sides of the yard and ahead stood a large manor house made of yellow moss-covered stone. Tall, curtained windows glowed with light and a small lamp hung from underneath a columned portico, illuminating an imposing front door.

The crooks marched me into a wide hall. The walls were panelled in dark oak and hung with shields and crossed swords; a chandelier twinkled from the ceiling high above and in front of me was a curving staircase rising to a wide upper landing. At various intervals around the hall stood full sets of gleaming armour. *Wow*, I thought. *These reprobates have come into a bit of money, and I bet they didn't earn one penny piece of it!*

On either side of the hall was a set of double doors and Twitch, having shaken the rain from his umbrella and changed his muddy shoes for a pair of highly patterned silk slippers, went and knocked on the doors to our right.

'Come!' a voice rang out from the other side, and at the sound of it the hairs on the back of my neck bristled. *No*, I thought. *Not him!*

Twitch opened the door into a large and comfortable study. The walls were lined with books; dark red curtains hung down to the floor and a fire crackled in a huge fireplace. Above the fireplace was the stuffed head of a gruesome creature, mounted on a plaque and staring down at us with glassy eyes. It looked like a strange cross between a hellish hound and a sharp-fanged tiger, and was labelled, THE DEMON OF DARKMOOR, BAGGED BY THE SQUIRE.

THE DEMON OF DARKMOOR
BAGGED BY THE SQUIRE

A large desk stood at an angle in one corner of the room. Behind it stood a red leather chair, its high back facing the room and hiding its occupant from view. *Please don't be him*, I thought, my heart pounding and my palms starting to sweat.

'A surprise guest for you, sir,' said Twitch, bowing theatrically and fluttering a lace hanky in his right hand.

The chair span round and there sat the worst, most devious, heartless, crookedest, sneaky, snaky, two-faced villain I've ever encountered: Joseph Craik, the one-time pirate turned thief-taker I'd first met with the Perfumed Pirates. His balding, bony skull was wrapped in a red spotted kerchief and his stubbly, scarred face was thrust aggressively forward as he stared at me with a rheumy eye.

Craik jumped to his feet, his jaw dropping open in astonishment before curling into a nasty sneer. 'Well, well; look what the cat threw up. If it ain't the detestable hairball that is Charlie Small,' he hissed through his blackened, stumpy teeth. 'Oh, life can't get much better than this! I've got untold riches; a magnificent mansion to call my own; a gang of the most callous crooks in the annals of crime and now *you* appear as if from nowhere.'

'Charlie Small!' cried Craik

With a satisfied sigh he sat down again and, leaning back in his chair and placing his rough shoes on the highly polished desk, fixed me with a glowering stare from his one good eye.

'So, what are you up to, you little puke-stain?' his menacing voice rumbled as he scratched the lousy stubble beneath the dirty bandana that covered his head.

I couldn't believe it. After all my adventures, I was back in the grip of my most hated enemy.

Craik's Tale Boo! Hiss!

'I'm not up to anything!' I squeaked.

'So, you turning up at our secret hideout just after we've pulled off some of the biggest bank raids in history is a coincidence, is it?' scoffed Craik, rising from his seat again and looming over his desk at me like a psychopathic headmaster. 'Try pulling the other one, you gnat.'

'It's the truth. I'm on my way home, if it's any of your business,' I said, trying to sound brave but failing miserably. Out of all the enemies I'd met on my travels, Craik was the one I feared most. He is as heartless as the devil.

'So, still trying to get back home are you?' he said. 'Surely you must realize by now that you're on a hidin' to nothin'?' Then, turning to his henchmen, he said, 'You've all met Charlie Small before, but what you don't know, me hearties, is that he comes from another world. Quite literally, another time and place.'

'Oh really! I always thought he was a bit of a weirdo, but you can't expect us to buy that,' said Twitch.

'*Whaaat?* Are you doubtin' me, you simpering cissy?' cried Craik thumping the table in sudden fury.

Twitch jumped back as if he'd been slapped. 'N-n-no boss, I wouldn't d-dream of it,' he stammered.

'Tell 'em, Charlie. Ain't it the truth?'

'You know it's true,' I said. 'You've already been there. It was you that dragged me back into this world after I'd finally managed to escape.'

'I said I'd track you to the ends of the earth and beyond and I always keep me promises, boy,' growled Craik ominously. 'No one steals from me and gets away with it. You robbed me, burgled my house, destroyed my power in the

Underworld and sank my galleon. By all the laws of pirate revenge, you shouldn't still be around. Well, that's a mistake I will soon put right.'

'How did you do it; how *did* you cross over into my world?' I asked.

Craik smirked, took something from a shelf behind him and sat back down again. 'Do you know what this is, Charlie?' he said, placing a stone bottle on the table.

'Where did you get that?' I gasped, immediately recognizing the onyx urn that contained a terrible Smoke Demon.

'A mad old Potentate gave it to me in return for his life,' said Craik with a terrible sneer. 'He begged and begged – said it contained a genie – but I didn't believe in such things so I made him walk the plank anyway. Ha! I can still hear his pathetic cries for mercy.'

'That was nice of you,' I said.

'He was of no concern,' said Craik, waving a hand dismissively through the air. 'You might not have known it, Charlie, but I was hot on your heels, anchored off the coast of the Forest

(See my Journal The Mummy's Tomb)

76

of Skulls, when word was sent that you had escaped down a secret tunnel back to your own world. I was furious; at the last minute you had given me the slip. Then I remembered this bottle and thought it was worth a try.' He held up the urn and gave it a shake. 'I took the top off and, lo and behold, a swirling spirit billowed out! I made a bargain with him, just like in the fairy stories – his freedom for three wishes.'

'What did you wish for?' I asked.

'Wish number one – set the genie free,' said the thief-taker. 'That was the deal. My second wish was to get into your world so I could grab you, you interfering worm.'

'And your third wish?' I asked.

'Well, that was *meant* to be for untold riches, but then I found I had to use my last wish to get back to my own world, curses!' growled Craik. 'Another way you've foiled my plans, Charlie Small. Never mind, you're here now and I can finally finish you off. Lock him up, Ham.'

'In the tower, sir?' asked Horatio Ham.

'Of course not. That's already occupied. Bung him in the cellar,' snarled Craik. Ham grabbed me by the scruff of the neck and manhandled me towards the door.

'Just a minute,' growled Craik, standing up and planting his hands on the table. 'Bring him back 'ere.'

Oh, jeepers, what now? I wondered as I was shoved back towards Craik's desk.

'You say you're on your way home. How on earth do you propose to get there?' he asked suspiciously.

'Oh, um, you know, just look around until I find a way,' I said lamely.

'Why don't I believe you, you mendacious maggot? *Search him!*' said Craik.

'No!' I cried as Twitch rummaged in my pockets and Ham ripped off my rucksack, turning the contents out onto the table. *Please don't find it; please don't find it,* I said to myself over and over.

'Aha!' cried Tristram Twitch, pulling my precious map from my back pocket. 'What's this?'

'Hand it over,' snapped Craik. He unfolded the paper and studied it carefully. For a long while he didn't say a word.

'So you were just gonna look around, were yer?' he said eventually. 'Do you know what this is, men?' he asked.

'No!' they all replied.

'It's a detailed map of where to cross over into Charlie's world,' he said, slapping the desk in triumph. 'You know what that means don't you, me little scabs?'

'Yeah,' said Ham.

'Sure,' agreed Twitch and Belcher. 'Actually, no!' they admitted.

'It means, numbskulls, that we can all travel into Charlie's world, pull off the most audacious heists in the annals of crime and then escape back here to absolute safety. It's the perfect getaway; no one will ever be able to find us!' said Craik, crossing his arms and smiling a horrible, greedy smile.

'Brilliant!' cried Craik's gang of goons.

'Give it back,' I murmured, almost too shocked and disappointed to talk. I had lost the most important document in the world to the meanest crook of all time.

'Is he still here?' bellowed Craik, looking up at me. 'Get him out of me sight. I'll deal with him in the morning.'

Ham swept my explorer's kit back into my rucksack, put it under his arm and then pushed me out of the room. He steered me down a long, wide passage that led from the imposing hall and into a large, old-fashioned kitchen. Gleaming copper pans hung from a bar over the black range; cabbages and turnips were piled on the work surface and a great side of bacon hung from a hook in one of the beams.

Horatio Ham opened a door in the far corner of the kitchen, revealing a staircase leading down into blackness. He pushed me inside.

'Here, you can keep this rubbish, boy,' he said, throwing my rucksack at me with such force that I lost my footing and fell backwards down the stairs, tumbling over and over until I landed with a crack on a hard, cobbled floor.

'Ooops, sorry . . . not!' laughed the greasy great twit and he slammed and bolted the door.

'Ouch! Let me out, you goon,' I yelled, rubbing the back of my aching head, but the thick cellar walls of the old building soaked up my voice like a sponge.

Well, I thought to myself. *You*

wanted somewhere to spend the night and that's exactly what you've got.

In The Cellar

Shining my torch around, I can see that I am in a small, low-ceilinged room hanging with swathes of dusty cobwebs. The walls and floor are made of solid stone and the thick door at the top of the stairs is the only entrance. It's been bolted from the other side, so I can't even use my skeleton-finger key to try and pick the lock.

There is one other opening into the cellar: a small, soot-smeared hole at the top of the outer wall that looks out at ground-level. It's no wider than my shoulders and is barred with a couple of thick iron rods set into the stone. I've tried to cut through them with my megashark's tooth, but after a solid hour's sawing it's hardly made a mark. I'm well and truly trapped.

There are a few old trunks stacked along one wall and I decided they would make a good bed. I'm stretched out on them now, writing up my journal and trying to think of ways to escape.

I'm pretty sure what Craik has in mind for me in the morning: he's always boasted about how he's going to see me hang from his portable gallows, and he's come close to it on more than one occasion.

It's really spooky down here; my torch casts deep black shadows in the corners of the room and I can see things crawling about in the cobwebs. Ugh! I hate spiders – I hope they don't crawl over me during the night . . . Hello, what's that noise? There's a horrible hissing sound coming from the coal-hole. I'd better go and investigate; I do hope it's not a humungous hairy-legged spider!

I'll write more, later – *if* I'm still around, that is.

Later

Well, would you believe it? I've just had a visit from one of the strangest characters I've ever met.

'Pssst,' I heard. 'Pssst!'

I crept over to the barred hole at the top of the wall and peered up. Caught in the glow of a lamp was one of the odd figures I'd seen working on the land before I'd been nabbed. A floppy hat was pulled down low over his long, lugubrious face, which had an unhealthy green pallor; his lips were grey and the 'whites' of his eyes a deep pink.

'Prisoner wait?' he said in a slow drawl. Then, to my amazement, he stuck his feet between the bars.

'What are you doing? You'll get stuck,' I whispered urgently, but the stranger ignored me.

He was as malleable as toothpaste and squeezed his shins, then his thighs, his chest and finally his shoulders through the gap. It was the strangest thing I've ever seen. It was as if he had no bones at all. With a plop he landed on the floor beside me and held out a very long, limp hand.

'Walt?' he enquired.

'No, Charlie. My name's Charlie Small,' I said, shaking his hand and shuddering slightly. It was very cold and clammy.

'My name's Walt?' asked the strange man slowly.

'I don't know, is it?' I asked, slightly puzzled.

'It is?' he replied. Then I understood: he said everything as if he were asking a question, which was very confusing.

'Pleased to meet you, Walt, but how did you do that?' I asked, pointing at the bars.

Walt

'I'm a Moor's Man?' said Walt. 'My people have lived on Darkmoor for centuries? The damp and the moisture has permeated our bones, making them as bendy as a switch of willow?'

'Really?' I said, astounded. 'You're running a huge risk coming here, you know. I'm being held prisoner by a horrible man called Craik.'

'We're all Craik's prisoners?' said Walt in his

slow, languid manner. His movements were slow too, as if he were underwater. 'We are made to work our own land and give him all our crops?'

'Why, what's he up to?' I asked.

'Don't know?' said Walt. 'Why are you being held?'

'Oh, I'm an old enemy of Joseph Craik,' I said. 'We go way back and he has sworn to see me hang. I reckon that's exactly what he's got planned for me at sunrise.'

'Oh, not long now?' said Walt, staring up to where the coal-hole was already showing a faint pink glow in the sky. 'I'll go and get help?'

'Oh, thanks, Walt, thanks so much,' I said as the tall man lifted his arms slowly, grabbed the bars and gradually pulled himself from the ground, squeezing through the gap as if he were a slimy slug. 'But please hurry!' I added as he languidly turned to look back down through the bars at me and give a slow wave.

'Don't worry?' he said, and with that he loped off into the looming dawn as if he were off on a leisurely stroll. Don't worry! That was easy for him to say. It wasn't him who was for it, and at the rate he was going he wouldn't even reach the end of the drive by noon, let alone get help!

I don't know what's going to happen, but I'm not holding out much hope of a rescue if Walt's pals are all as slow and slothful as he is. Don't get me wrong, he seems like a very nice man, but he could do with a rocket behind him!

Appointment With Doom! Yikes!

Yahoo! Once again I've managed to escape from that weasel-faced twit, Joseph Craik, and you'll never guess where I am now! I'm still on the moor, in the middle of a thorny hideout and in the company of – no! I'm rushing ahead of myself. Let me explain *exactly* what happened.

As the sun began to rise, a shaft of bright sunlight entered through the coal-hole, illuminating the cellar. Now I could see more clearly, I quickly searched my prison to see if I'd overlooked an escape route, but no such luck; I was in a solid subterranean vault. I opened some of the trunks, trying to find something I could use to defend myself but, apart from some gross, scuttling spiders, they were empty.

Then with a clatter and a clang the door at the top of the steps flew open and Belcher came huffing and puffing down the stairs.

'Good mornin', dear boy,' he said, a sneering smile creasing his fat, flabby face. 'Craik has asked if you would kindly join him in the stable yard.'

'Do I have any choice?' I asked.

'None at all,' said Belcher, his jowls wobbling with mirth. 'Come on, let's be having you.' And he herded me upstairs, through the hall and out into the forecourt. Just as I'd expected, Craik's portable noose was ready and waiting in the centre, its loop of deadly rope spinning slowly in the breeze.

There was no sign of Craik, but his cronies were standing around chatting and laughing. As well as the goons I'd already seen, I also recognized some of their henchmen who I'd met on earlier adventures. There were Twitch's men, Syd and Perce; Belcher's brigands, Sidekick and Ramon; and Horatio Ham's right-hand man, Mad Marshall Mickey McKay. I gave an involuntary shiver. What a lovely bunch!

'Oh, shucks! Look, it's Charlie Small,' said Sidekick. 'What you doin' here?'

'I think I'm here for a hanging,' I said, desperately looking round for a sign of Walt and

(See my Journal Frostbite Pass)

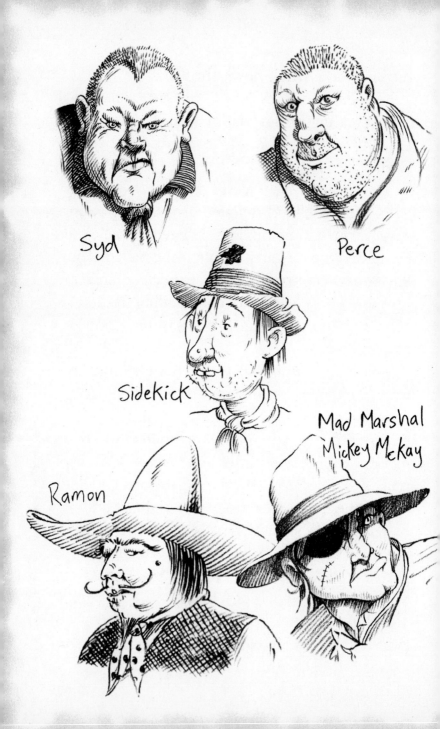

Syd

Perce

Sidekick

Ramon

Mad Marshal
Mickey McKay

his rescue party. Beyond the gates I could see along the tunnel through the copse to a stretch of moorland beyond. There was no sign of anyone but my captors and, apart from a horse shuffling and snorting in one of the nearby stables, all was quiet.

'Oh, neat! That's what *we're* here for,' chuckled Sidekick. 'So, who is getting hanged, exactly?' He wasn't the brightest of sparks!

'That would be me,' I said.

'Oh, neat,' chuckled Sidekick again.

'Glad we could be here to witness your demise, Charlie,' said the great bruiser, Syd. He had obviously patched things up with his wimpy boss. The last time I'd seen Syd, he was chasing a terrified Twitch and threatening to ring his scrawny neck!

'It's not over yet,' I said, although I had to admit things looked pretty bleak.

'Right, stop all this chit-chat,' bellowed Craik, suddenly appearing from the manor house and marching across the forecourt, his boots crunching on the cobbles and a black velvet coat billowing out behind him like a vampire's cape.

The gang instantly stopped talking and stood nervously to attention. They were petrified of their ruthless leader.

'Let's get this job over with. I want this irritating pustule out of my life without delay,' Craik continued. 'I'm hungry for me breakfast!'

I gulped – it looked like my number was well and truly up. There was no sign of help. The strange Moor's Man, Walt, had let me down.

The Hawk!

As Craik approached, the restless horse kicked at his stable door and whinnied. 'What's wrong with the 'orses? Go check them out, Perce.'

'Yes, sir,' said Perce, but as he started towards the stable door, it suddenly flew open with a crash. A jet-black horse burst out, reared up with its front hooves flailing the air and then galloped straight towards us, throwing back its head and neighing wildly. On the back of the horse, cape flowing out like a pair of wings, sat a strange and awesome figure.

'Stand fast, you devils,' came a raucous squawk and I gasped in astonishment, for the rider was a massive bird of prey! Fierce yellow eyes stared from its feathery face and its curved

beak looked as sharp as a scythe.

'It's the Hawk!' screamed Twitch and he fell shivering to the cobbles. Perce was knocked aside and the others stood around in dumb surprise, as the Hawk reached down and dragged me up by the scruff of my neck onto the back of the galloping horse.

At the same time, Craik drew his pistol and aimed directly at me. With a twitch of the reins, the Hawk turned the horse and kicked the pistol from his grasp, just as it went off. The bullet whizzed past my ear and the gun span across the yard, landing with a clatter.

'Don't just stand there, you vermin. Get your guns and get after them!' bellowed Craik, and as the Hawk urged our horse forward and we galloped for the gates, the gang ran to saddle their mounts.

I held on to the Hawk, its cape flapping in my face, unable to see a thing. The horse's hooves clattered on the cobbles, shooting sparks into the air. We went crunching down the gravel drive, through the leafy tunnel and then, with a magnificent leap to clear a dyke, we were thumping across the springy moor grass and splashing through mist-shrouded ponds.

'Where are you taking me?' I shouted above the rushing of the wind. 'Did Walt send you?' For I had no idea if this hook-nosed creature was my rescuer, or whether I'd just been snaffled for a snack. The Hawk didn't say a word but carried on riding. I didn't dare jump from the galloping horse– so I hung on for dear life.

We leaped streams and rocky outcrops; we skirted mires and galloped under rock arches until, all of a sudden, the Hawk pulled the snorting horse up and jumped to the ground. I stared in wonder as the feathered fiend ran up the side of a ridge and stood atop an enormous granite rock. Now I could see the thing had the head of an eagle, but the body of a human! It wore yellow leather gauntlets with long talons and a pair of knee-length feathered boots. Suddenly it threw out its arms, the wing-shaped cape billowing behind it, and let out an ear-piercing screech.

'Yeeaark!' the Hawk screamed, taunting the following felons. Silhouetted against the stormy-looking sky, it was an awesome and scary sight.

In the distance I could hear the rumble of horses' hooves as Craik's men came a-galloping. I heard the crack of a gun and the Hawk leaped down as a bullet ricocheted from the rock with a whistle. They were closer than I'd thought!

The Hawk's Nest

In a single bound the Hawk was astride the horse and we were galloping across the moor once again. We rode like the wind, our horse's hooves invisible in the blanket of mist that lay close to the ground. Bullets whistled past us as we weaved a path through some low, fat Tors. We rounded a corner and in the shelter of the rocks, the Hawk slid from the saddle again, drawing a sword from its scabbard and banging the hilt on some wide slabs on the ground.

Hold on, that's my *sword,* I thought as the great bird leaped up beside me once more. As the gang of crooks came galloping amongst the Tors, shouting and whooping like wild things, the slabs at our feet flipped back and a host of wartbogs came crawling out. The Hawk kicked our stallion and we shot away as the growling moor monsters went snapping ferociously towards the crooks. The spooked horses reared up and threw their riders to the ground.

'Oof!' we heard as the crooks landed with hefty thumps. Then, 'Get off you . . . ouch!' as the wartbogs attacked.

'Yeeaark!' the Hawk screamed again as we raced away across the moor.

'No!' cried one of the crooks, followed by a *splash!* as he was driven into a nearby mire. We were too far away to see who it was, and the crooks were too busy fending off the bog freaks to follow us.

A couple of miles further on, we came to a wall of yellow gorse bushes about two and a half metres high. With a loud screech the Hawk steered the stallion straight towards it.

'That's way too high to jump,' I cried in a panic, but at the last minute a section of the tangled wall rolled back and we galloped inside. The hedge closed behind us and I found myself in a small clearing within a ring of very thick, very thorny gorse. The Hawk pulled the stallion to a halt, leaped down from the saddle and reached up to help me down.

As the creature's hands grabbed me under my arms and pulled me forward, I drew my face away from the vicious beak, scared I was going to be ripped into slices. Then, as I was placed on the ground, the Hawk reached up, grabbed either side of its feathery neck and yanked. Slowly the bird's head started to come off!

Whoa, this is weird, I thought as, with a final tug, the head popped off, and there stood a girl about fourteen years old, shaking out her long, brown hair.

'Phew, that's better,' she said. 'It gets so hot in there! Welcome to the Hawk's Nest, Charlie Small.'

'You're a girl!' I said. 'And you know my name.'

'Oh, well done. I can see nothing gets past you,' she said, taking off her clawed gloves. 'Of course I know your name, Walt told me.'

'I thought you were . . . I mean, the hawk's head is so realistic, I just thought . . .' I said moronically.

'You thought I really was a birdman?' laughed the girl. She was very pretty, with a small turned-up nose, the palest skin and rosy cheeks. Under the winged cloak she was wearing purple velvet knickerbockers, feathered boots to her knees and a bright red waistcoat.

'Yes, if you must know,' I said, starting to feel rather foolish. 'I did think you were some sort of mythical beast. A scary one too.'

'Well, if I fooled you, it's done its job,' she said with satisfaction.

'But why are you wearing a falcon headpiece and why are you living here of all places?' I asked, looking around her hideout. It was clean and tidy, but a very ramshackle affair.

On the far side of the clearing, up against the tangled branches of the gorse ring, was a row of very low dome-shaped dwellings. They were like giant turtle shells woven from willow, and looked as if there'd be just enough room to crawl underneath them.

Outside the huts, I was surprised to see a group of the tall, green-skinned Moor's Men sitting cross-legged with their wives and children. The men wore trousers the colour and texture of moss and the women wore full, long khaki-coloured skirts. Some had been weaving baskets from rushes, others were preparing food, but now they all turned to stare at me with vacant looks on their long faces.

'Don't worry, he's a friend,' said the girl, and without uttering a word they returned to their work. Then to me she said, 'I'll tell you everything later, Charlie. My name's Kitty, by the way. Kitty Hawksmoor.'

'Pleased to meet you, Kitty, and thanks so much for rescuing me from crazy Craik and his gang,' I said.

'Don't mention it. Any enemy of Craik's is a friend of mine,' said the girl. 'Now, how about a bite to eat?'

At the mention of food, my tummy gurgled. 'Oh, yes please,' I said.

Uninvited Guests

I followed Kitty to a hut where a Moor's Woman was cooking something in a pot over the glowing embers of a fire. Above the fire was an unusual contraption – a little wooden roof with a tube coming from the top that curled over and went into the ground.

'What's that for?' I asked.

'That's the chimney,' explained Kitty. 'We can't afford to let any smoke drift above the height of the gorse wall in case one of Craik's cronies spots it. The smoke is trapped under the roof, feeds along the tube and disperses in the cracks and crevices of the bedrock.'

The odd chimney over the fire

Smoke goes into ground →

Smoke

'Ingenious,' I said. 'So what's —'

'Shush?' interrupted one of the Moor's Men, cupping his long hand around a droopy ear. 'Somethin's comin'?' He talked in the same questioning manner as Walt.

'What is it?' I whispered, straining my ears, but I couldn't hear a thing.

'Visitors?' said the man in a lazy drawl. 'Seven of 'em?' Then I heard it too – the sound of approaching horses.

'Whoa!' came a cry, and I immediately recognized Craik's voice. 'Search this place; rip it apart. They might be hiding anywhere in these bushes. If you find 'em, finish 'em.'

We held our breaths as the crooks dismounted and started their search. They were only a couple of metres away, but the bushes were so thick we couldn't see them. Then the branches started to shake as the gang tried to force their way into the thicket, and my heart began to pound in dread. I needn't have worried though – the Hawk had chosen her nest well.

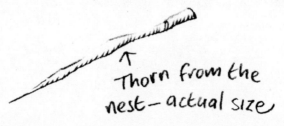

Thorn from the nest – actual size

'Yeeow!' complained Horatio Ham. 'These thorns are lethal. I've been submerged up to my neck in a quagmire, and now I'm being punctured.'

'Hot diggety,' cried Mad Marshall Mickey McKay. 'There's no way anyone could hide amongst this stuff, boss. It's like barbed wire.'

'Don't talk rot – out of my way,' yelled Craik. 'This'll do the trick.' And the bushes shuddered violently as he attacked them with a thick, fallen branch.

Then, 'Ouch!' he cried. 'Hell's fire! It's impregnable. We're wasting our time here; let's get back to the manor. There's only Twitch and Perce guarding the Squire.'

As we heard this, I saw Kitty physically bristle and her eyes flashed with anger.

Tall Tales And Roasted Bugs Yuk!

The horsemen galloped away and we began to breathe more easily.

'Grub's up?' said the Moor's Woman tending the fire.

Goody, grub at last, I thought. Then my heart

sank as she took the lid off her pot and tipped a pile of big, brown beetle-like bugs onto a plate. They were the size of mobile phones and covered with a hard, shiny carapace.

'I hope yer like Moorland Bugs?' she said, licking her long, spatulate fingers. "'Cause it's all we've got?'

As I stared in disbelief at the crusty alien-looking creature, my tummy did a flip. *Surely no one is going to eat these disgusting things,* I thought. But Kitty sat down and tucked in right away.

'Come on, Charlie. What are you waiting for?' she said, with a humorous twinkle in her eye. I picked a bug up and gave it a cautious sniff; I put out my tongue and gave it a quick lick then, closing my eyes, I took a bite. It was very crunchy on the outside, but creamy in the middle and it was absolutely delicious; strong and tangy, and

Fancy a nice baked Moorland bug?

a bit like eating crisps dipped in mayonnaise. It was a meal fit for a king.

Kitty introduced me to the Moor's People. There was Dwight and Scrumpy, Zeke, Mossy, Hortense, Verdant – oh, I can't remember all their names! They were all as lethargic and slow as Walt had been, but very friendly.

'So, why are you hiding out in the middle of the moor and what are Craik and his gang doing living in that great big house?' I asked, giving a small burp and taking another baked bug.

'That's Hawksmoor Hall. It's where I live with my dad, the Squire,' said Kitty. 'The Moor's Folk are our tenant farmers.'

'Wow! You lucky thing,' I said. 'I'd love to live in a place like that.'

'So would I,' said Kitty with a wry smile. 'About two months ago I came home from boarding school for the holidays, but as I rode up the drive I was stopped by Walt. He told me that Dad had been taken prisoner by a bunch of ne'er-do-wells who'd taken over the Hall. They had banished all the Moor's Folk who lived on our estate, apart from Walt and a few others they'd kept on as serfs. They've been there nearly a year now. I was so livid I was ready to ride up to the house and kick them out, but Walt warned me how dangerous they are. Especially their leader.'

'Yes, Craik is a nasty piece of work,' I agreed. 'What are they doing here anyway?'

'They're lying low after a series of daring robberies,' said Kitty. 'There isn't another house for a hundred miles, making it a perfect hideout. So I had to come and live on the moor. I discovered this clump of impenetrable thorn bushes and with the help of some Moor's Men, hacked into it with machetes and made a clearing in the middle. It took weeks and we got covered in scratches, but we managed it.'

'So, what's with the Hawk's head?' I asked.

'Simple – I don't want Craik's lot to know who I am. I've been busy upsetting their plans and generally making a nuisance of myself, hoping they'd give up and move on,' Kitty explained. 'If they knew I was the Squire's daughter they might take it out on Dad, so I became the Hawk, terror of the moor! Also, it looks pretty cool, don't you think? Hortense made it for me.'

'It's brilliant – and very scary-looking,' I agreed. 'I'd never guess you were just a girl.'

'Just a girl – *just* a girl?' cried Kitty. 'You're as

bad as my dad. He sent me off to finishing school to make me into the perfect young lady. I mean, how boring is that? Little does he know, Miss Prim's Academy for Demure Young Damsels is a very special finishing school. They teach karate, jujitsu, fencing, shooting and unarmed combat. Come on, I'll show you if you like.'

Just a girl?

'No, it's OK, I didn't mean – *whoa!*' I cried as Kitty grabbed me by the wrist and sent me flying through the air to land with a thump on the ground. As I got to my feet, gasping for breath, she grabbed me again and threw me over her shoulder as if I were a rag doll.

'Oof!' I cried. 'OK, OK, I believe you!'

'Don't ever call me *just* a girl,' said Kitty, her face all flushed and angry. 'Now, perhaps you'd better tell me what *you're* doing here.'

I humbly took my seat next to the Moor's Men again. They hadn't shown a flicker of interest as I'd been sent whizzing round the camp.

'Fancy another bug?' asked Scrumpy as if nothing had happened.

'Yeah, thanks,' I said, my pride a little bruised.

As evening started to draw in, I told Kitty and the others all about my crazy adventures, how I'd ended up on Darkmoor and how I'd lost my precious map to the great bully, Craik.

'I have to get it back,' I said. 'I just have to.'

'Perhaps we could join forces and help each other,' said Kitty. 'We can drive Craik away and get your map back at the same time. Sorry about beating you up, by the way.'

'Beating me up, I don't think . . .' I began. Then I remembered just how easily she had sent me flying through the air and decided to bite my tongue. 'Yeah, well I s'pose you had good reason,' I said. 'You're right; I think we would make a pretty good team. Watch out, Craik, that's all I can say!'

It's late at night now, and I'm curled up beneath a horse blanket under one of the low woven domes, ready for sleep. The air is filled with the gentle, gurgling snores of the moor folk,

my tummy is full of Moorland Bugs and I'm as
snug as a bug in a rug! Much to my surprise, I
found that Kitty had discovered my hiding place
up on the escarpment and already retrieved my
Air-rider. She also gave me back the pirate's
scimitar. Tomorrow, Kitty and I are going
to Hawksmoor Hall to spy out the land. I'm
tingling with excitement. I'll write more later.

Hawksmoor Hall

A rosy sun was still low in the sky and mist
swirled knee-high around us as we left camp the
next morning. Kitty was wearing the fearsome
feathered hawk's head again and insisted I call
her Hawk when she was in disguise. It is really
life-like and it's difficult to picture the slight,
pretty girl underneath.

I was on the Air-rider, following her big black
stallion, Nightmare. I left my pirate scimitar
back at the nest with the moor folk – we were
going to have to do a lot of creeping about, and
it would only get in my way. We reached a point
on the high ridge that overlooked one side of
the Hall, and Hawk dismounted.

The Hawk on her horse, Nightmare

'We'd better leave our mounts here,' she said. 'We'll have to be awfully careful from here on in.'

I looked down at the manor house. It was a big sprawling pile, three storeys high with battlements along the roof and a tower at the rear. Then I remembered something Craik had said.

'Hey, Kitty, sorry, I mean Hawk, I've just thought – I think I might know where your dad is being kept,' I said.

'Where?' said Hawk, her eyes flashing with excitement.

'Craik put me in the cellar because he said the tower was already occupied,' I explained.

'The tower – of course, it's the perfect place!' said Hawk. 'That explains why Walt and his chums haven't seen sight or sound of him. There's only one way in, up a winding narrow stairway, and it's virtually unscalable from the outside.'

'Oh, I think I might be able to climb it,' I said, trying not to sound too smug. 'I was taught to climb by gorillas and I spent ages in the rigging of a pirate ship.'

'Really?' said Hawk, looking amazed. 'And I thought you were *just* a boy!'

'Ha ha,' I said. 'Come on, let's go and see if we can find your dad. We might even be able to rescue him today.'

One of the gorilla climbing instructors

We crouched low, darting from rock to bush, to clumps of tall grass for cover. The ground was springy and squelched slightly underfoot. As we got closer, we got down on our bellies and crawled forward until we came to the wide moat that ran all around the outside of the building.

'What now?' I whispered.

'We'll have to wade across,' said Hawk. 'It's not very deep.'

'You're joking!' I said, but Hawk was already easing herself down into the muddy water. I took off my trainers, jammed them into my rucksack and rolled up my jeans.

Ugh! It was cold and the mud on the bottom of the moat squidged between my toes. It was also a lot deeper than Hawk had thought and the water was soon up to our waists. Then the bottom disappeared altogether and we had to swim for the far side. We crawled out onto a steep, narrow bank that sloped up to the wall of the manor house. I was soaking wet and covered in slimy duckweed.

'Sorry about that, we must have had some heavy rains while I was away at school,' said Hawk.

We were perched just below a wide, diamond-paned window and I could hear some noise coming from inside the manor.

'Shush!' I whispered pointing at the window, and I carefully stood up and peered over the sill. The crooks were sitting around a long table having their breakfast. They didn't go without food, that's for sure! They had ham and kedgeree, sausages and eggs, devilled kidneys and a huge flagon of wine that they passed around, slurping and chewing and talking all at the same time.

'Good, they're busy eating. No one should disturb us,' I whispered and we climbed awkwardly along the steep bank at the base of the wall, turned a corner and shuffled along the back wall to the fat round tower. Here the bank was much wider, and we stood staring up at the tower, which climbed high above the rest of the building. At the very top were a few narrow slit windows.

The Squire

The Tower

'Wow! It's high!' I said.

'I told you it was a tough climb,' said Hawk. 'Don't tell me you're going to wimp out now.'

'Of course not,' I said with a gulp. The wall rose vertically up and the stone building blocks were so well cut that there wasn't a single foothold. There was some ivy growing to about halfway up though, and I grabbed hold and pulled myself from the ground. 'You wait here,' I said. 'I'll go and see if there's anybody in there.'

'But the ivy will only take you part of the way,' said Hawk.

'Don't worry about that,' I said and began my climb. I soon reached the top of the ivy where I raised my arm and fired my little wristband anchor. It shot skyward, trailing its wire behind it, and curved over the top of the crenulated wall where it fell with a clatter onto the tower's roof. I gave it a tug, checking it was firmly anchored, and then started the whirring motor that reeled the wire in.

As it did so, I was hauled up the side of the building as if I were in an invisible lift, and I heard Hawk give a little cry of surprise. I was pulled right to the dizzying top, where I clambered over the wall and dropped to the tower's roof on the other side. I unhooked the anchor from the battlement and took out the length of vine from my explorer's kit. I tied this to one of the raised blocks of the crenulated wall and threw the other end over the side so it dangled close to one of the windows.

Then, giving Hawk a thumbs-up, I swung myself over the wall and, making sure not to look down, lowered myself quietly and gently onto the wide sill of the window below. In front of me was the dark rectangle of the window; behind, a sheer twenty-five metre drop to the moat. There was no glass in the narrow slit so I edged myself forwards and peered inside, listening for the sound of someone moving about, some breathing or a cough. But it was completely silent.

I couldn't see a thing at first, but as my eyes adjusted to the gloom I made out a dusty, circular room. There was an untidy bed to my right and a rickety chair pulled up to an old desk that was covered with sheets of paper and an empty breakfast plate. A frayed tapestry hung on the wall opposite me, but there was no sign of the room's occupant. I jumped down from the sill and . . . *oof!* I was leaped on and wrestled to the ground.

'Get off!' I cried in a hoarse whisper, but my attacker clamped a strong arm around my neck and hauled me to my feet. He was standing behind me and, struggle as I might, I couldn't turn to see who it was. 'Let go,' I croaked as the arm tightened around my throat.

'Who are you and why are you creeping about in my room?' said a man. 'Quick now, or I'll squeeze you 'til you crack! I've had as much as I can stand.'

'Can't talk!' I croaked. 'Too tight.' The man loosened his grip a little. 'That's better!' I gasped. 'My name's Charlie Small.'

I was immediately spun around and I found myself staring at a small, tubby and swarthy man with a bulbous red nose, small blue eyes, a grey goatee beard and a head of wild, wiry hair that made him look as mad as a hatter!

'And what are you doing here, Charlie Small?' he asked breathlessly.

'Are you Squire Hawksmoor?' I asked.

'Maybe, maybe not.'

'I'm a friend of Kitty's and I've come to help,' I said, and at the mention of Kitty's name, he let me go, fell to his knees and burst into tears.

'You know my Kitty?' he said in a pleading way, then just as quickly became angry again. 'How do I know this isn't some sort of trick dreamed up by Craik? Have you nabbed her as well?' he barked, grabbing me roughly by the shoulders and shaking me.

'It's no trick,' I cried, my voice vibrating as he shook me. 'Look out of the window if you don't believe me.' The Squire let me go and rushed so quickly to the window he nearly tipped out!

'There's no one there!' he gabbled. I joined him at the narrow slit, leaned out and looked down. He was right.

'She was there,' I said rather lamely.

'It *is* a trick, you swine,' he cried. 'Ooh, I'll tear you limb from limb, you little devil!' He pounced, but I was too quick for the roly-poly man.

'Won't Craik ever give up?' he gabbled, yanking at his wild, wiry hair and stalking around the cell like a caged tiger. 'What have you done with my daughter? Tell him I'll sign the deeds over to him if he just lets her go!'

What is he on about? I thought. *He's a complete loon!* Then I had an idea. I leaned back out of the window and let out a hawk's cry.

'*Eeeaaark!*' I screeched. '*Eeeaaark!*' Then, 'Look, there she is,' I cried as Hawk tiptoed around the base of the tower and peered up.

The Squire looked. 'Very funny, I don't think. What the heck is that, you double-crossing . . . ?'

Just then Kitty took the hawk's head off for a second and waved up at us. 'My goodness, it *is* her! What's she wearing that for?' gasped the Squire. 'Kitty!' he bellowed out of the window.

'Shush!' I said. 'Craik will hear you, and then he *will* nab Kitty.'

'You'rerightI'msosorryIdidn'tbelieveyoubutI've beenstuckinthisroomforayearnowandIhaven'tseen alivingsoulexceptCraikandIthinkit'sstartingtogetto me,' said the Squire in a garbled whisper, his eyes shining wildly.

'Just calm down a bit,' I said and explained what Kitty had been up to and why she was in disguise.

'So, *she's* the Hawk that I've heard Craik moan about. Good for her. Did you know she foiled a robbery they'd been planning for months by putting thistle-heads under the gang's saddles? The poor horses went wild; Craik was thrown and nearly broke his neck before they'd even left the moor. I saw it all from my window. Laugh? It was better than a silent movie!'

'Yeah, she also held up Tristram Twitch when he was out in the fields and stole his gun, his sword and his favourite velvet knickerbockers. She left him standing in the rain in just his undies!' I laughed.

'That's my girl,' said the Squire proudly.

'So what were you on about, signing deeds for Craik?' I asked. 'What's he up to?'

'Craik is desperate to be the legal squire of Hawksmoor and has been trying to get me to sign all my property over to him – the house; the land; my fortune; everything. He's kept me up here in solitary on bread and water for the past year, but I refuse to sign. It's awful. You wouldn't know it to look at me, but I used to be quite portly!'

'Really?' I said, trying to sound surprised. 'Come on. There's no time like the present; let's see if we can get you out of here!'

A Leap Of Faith! (Geronimoooo...!)

I looked at the podgy Squire and then at the narrow window. There was no way he would fit through that. Perhaps I could pick the lock on the cell door with my skeleton finger key. I knelt down at the heavy door and, taking the bony finger from my rucksack, inserted it into the lock. I wiggled it until I felt it catch on the mechanism. But as I turned the finger to force the lock, I felt it snap. Flip! I'd broken the end off inside – and now I could hear footsteps clomping up the stairs.

'Someone's coming. See you later,' I whispered to the Squire as I darted across the room and hurled

The finger bone

myself headlong out of the window, grabbing the dangling rope mid-flight and shinning up to the roof. I could hear someone banging and rattling the cell door below. Then a crash as it finally burst open and I heard Craik's sneering voice.

'Been trying to break out have you?' he laughed at the Squire. 'You're wastin' yer time.

It's a tumbler lock and I keep the only key around my neck. Now, have you decided to sign over the deeds to the Hall, you gibbering nit?'

'No way, Craik,' said the Squire with a half-demented giggle. 'Things are afoot; the Hawk is on the prowl and she's not alone.'

No! I thought. *Don't give the game away!*

'What do you know of the Hawk – what's been going on here?' roared Craik, obviously unnerved. 'Come on, you crazy old loon, speak up!'

But just then a cry came from below.
'Eeeaaark!'

I looked over the parapet just as Craik's kerchief-covered skull appeared at the window beneath me. On the ground below, the Hawk, her mask back on, was standing with her arms raised. Belcher and Twitch had silently swum the moat and now had her covered her with their pistols.

'Ha! They've got the Hawk. So *that's* who tried to pick your lock!' growled Craik. Then he shouted to his men below. 'Stay where you are, lads, I'm on my way.'

Craik disappeared from the window and I heard the cell door slam shut and the click of the lock. I had to act quickly before Craik unmasked the Hawk and took her into custody.

I rammed the vine back in my rucksack, hooked the metal anchor on my wristband to the wall and jumped, letting the wire unravel as I fell. When I approached the top of the ivy, I pressed a button on the band and my descent slowed and then stopped. I had no way of unhooking the anchor at the top of the tower, so I undid the wristband and left it dangling as I quietly crawled down through the thick foliage. Soon I was perched just above Belcher, the tattoo-headed brigand.

'You just stay there, Hawk,' he was saying. 'Craik'll be here in a minute and you and your interfering ways will be over.'

'*Eeeaaark!*' I cried as I launched myself from the ivy and dropped onto Belcher, knocking the huge bandit to the ground. His gun went flying and the fat thief rolled off the bank, into the water. At the same time, the Hawk flew at Twitch in a soaring karate kick. His gun plopped into the moat and with a lightning-fast judo throw, the Hawk sent the whimpering Twitch in after it. *Splash!*

'Let's get out of here!' I yelled and we dived over the floundering felons and swam to the other bank. Dripping wet, we crawled out and ran for the open moor. Now, though, the other gang members had appeared from the front of the house and cut off our retreat. They were still chewing their breakfast and had come unarmed, apart from a few blunt butter knives, but Mad Mickey McKay, Syd, Perce, Gomez and Sidekick formed a semicircular wall of muscle around us and started to edge forward. If they thought they had us beaten, they were wrong, for now the Hawk really showed what she'd learned at finishing school and dived amongst them in a tornado spin.

She leaped and turned, seeming to hang suspended in the air for seconds as she kicked, chopped, parried and punched with an incredible display of martial arts. *Oof! Ouch! Argh!* Mad McKay crumpled to the ground after a karate chop. Syd landed with a bone-crunching thump after a judo throw, and Perce ended up sitting dazed and confused by a high-flying spinning kick. Gomez and Sidekick, who had been hanging back and looking very nervous, turned on their heels and ran for cover.

Then Craik appeared, riding his horse and brandishing two pistols. *Crack! Crack!* He let off a couple of shots and we dived to the ground in a roll. As we did so, Kitty's mask came off.

'Hah! You're just a girl!' Craik said, pulling his horse to a halt. 'And to think we thought you were some sort of avenging super-hero!'

Uh oh, you'll regret calling her just *a girl,* I thought.

'Say your prayers, little girly. You're about to meet your maker,' spat Craik, kicking his horse into a gallop. He came charging towards us with pistols blazing and the horse's reins clamped between his teeth.

'Ready for another swim?' asked Kitty, her face flushed with excitement.

'Sure!' I said.

'Then follow me,' she said and ran for the moat. As bullets zinged around us, we dived back into the muddy water and disappeared below the surface, just as Twitch and Belcher were managing to scramble out. It was hard to see Kitty through the murk, but she grabbed my hand and we kicked for the deep centre of the moat where a thick clump of reeds was growing. We forced our way between them and surfaced in the middle.

Swim For It!

We were completely hidden from view, but Craik had seen the reeds move.

'They're amongst the rushes,' he cried. 'Get them!' As some of the gang began wading into the moat, Craik fired a shot into the reeds. The bullet whistled past my shoulder as Kitty quickly snapped off two of the rushes, careful not to make a rustling sound. They were flexible and completely hollow.

'Use this as a snorkel and make for the bridge at the front of the manor,' she hurriedly whispered, bending a reed into a U-shape and handing it to me. Then, putting the other reed in her mouth, she was gone, swimming out of the reeds underneath the water. I watched her for a second; she was almost invisible. All I could see was the tip of the reed moving smoothly across the moat with a slight ripple in its wake. I put my homemade snorkel into my mouth, ducked under the water and followed.

The reed worked wonderfully well and I found I could breathe easily. My rucksack acted as a weight and kept me from bobbing to the surface as I followed the moat along the side of the manor. I could hear the faint, muffled yells of an increasingly angry Craik, and the splashes of the gang as they searched for us among the clump of rushes; we'd left just in time.

The bent reed made a good snorkel!

I followed the moat as it went round the front of the Hall, where I had to surface for a second to get my bearings in the murky water. Luckily there was no one at the front of the building, but I could hear Craik cursing his gang and firing his guns into the water in frustration. I submerged again and kicked for the low bridge that took the drive over the moat and into the forecourt. A minute later, I was under the arch and I surfaced to find Kitty waiting for me.

'What now?' I asked, coughing and spluttering as I accidentally swallowed a mouthful of water and duckweed. 'We can't stay here, they're bound to find us before long.'

'But they don't know about this,' said Kitty with a grin and she swam over to the inside of the bridge where it arched down into the water. She felt about under the surface. 'Here it is,' she said with a satisfied grin. 'Come and give me a hand.'

Just under the surface I felt a rusty iron lever and together we pushed it down. As Craik and some of his cronies came round the corner of the manor, still carefully scanning the moat, an oak panel on the underside of the bridge sprang open to reveal a small, dark chamber on the

other side. We dragged our sodden selves into it
and pulled the panel closed behind us.

I let out a sigh of relief. 'That was really
close,' I gasped. I was soaked from head to foot,
covered in slimy weed and shivering with cold.
'*Atishoo!* Oh brilliant, now I've caught a chill.'

'It could be worse, Charlie,' said Kitty starting
to shiver herself. 'We could've been shot as full
of holes as a colander. Anyway, we'll soon have
some dry clothes. This way.'

Kitty felt about on the back wall and pressed
a hidden button, making another panel slide
back. Beyond was a narrow set of wooden

steps. We squeezed ourselves into the small gap, climbed down them and found ourselves at the start of a long stone-clad tunnel.

'It leads under the moat, crosses beneath the courtyard and comes up inside the manor house,' said Kitty. 'It's an old escape route from the times of the Moor Wars. Come on.'

A Secret Room

We hurried along the tunnel. It was dark and smelled as damp and stale as a seaside cave. I flicked on my torch. It had stayed dry in my waterproof rucksack and its beam lit up the gloomy passage.

'Where does this tunnel come out?' I asked.

'You'll see, we're nearly there,' said Kitty. After a couple of hundred metres we came to another set of rickety, rotting steps. I followed Kitty to the top, where she opened a very narrow door and stepped through. I turned off my torch and followed her inside.

She lit a lamp and I saw that we were in a snug room with wood-panelled walls. The room was completely enclosed with no windows and, as far as I could see, no doorway other than the one we'd just come through. There were a few chairs, a table and a long cupboard at the far end.

'Where the heck are we?' I asked.

'Shush!' warned Kitty, standing on a chair and sliding back a small panel in the wall, about thirty centimetres square. Behind it was a dark, concave space with two eyeholes that showed as bright dots of light. 'We're in a secret room. Take a look!'

I put my head inside and peered through the holes. I was looking down on the study in which I'd been brought before Craik, and realized my

128

head was inside the Demon of Darkmoor's head that I'd seen mounted above the fireplace. Just below me was Craik's desk, littered with papers, and on top I could clearly see my precious map.

'Wow, it's brilliant!' I whispered, jumping down from the chair. 'How long have you known about this place?'

'Oh, I used to play in here when I was a nipper,' said Kitty. 'And I've been using it to spy on Craik; I overheard the gang planning their robberies and was able to foil a few, but I never learned where they were holding my dad.'

'And what is The Demon of Darkmoor?' I asked, pointing up at the head in the spy hatch.

'It was a legendary creature that used to roam the moor. It consumed sheep and horses and scores of poor Moor's Men before my great-great granddaddy finally put an end to its reign of terror with his trusty old blunderbuss,' said Kitty proudly.

'Gruesome! So, what shall we do now?' I asked, starting to shiver violently.

'First we'd better get changed into some dry clothes,' said Kitty opening the cupboard. There was a rail of clothes inside. 'It's where I used

129

to keep my dressing-up clothes when I was younger. I'm sure I'll have something to fit you.'

'You've got to be kidding,' I said, spying the line of dresses, skirts, and blouses. 'That's all girl's stuff. I'd rather stay wet, thanks. *Atishoo!*'

'There are some trousers here,' said Kitty, pulling out a pair of knee-length, green satin breeches and a very frilly shirt and waistcoat. 'Here put these on before you catch pneumonia. They used to be Dad's when he was younger.'

'Do I have to? *Atishoo!*' I sneezed, looking around for somewhere to change.

'It's all right, I'll turn my back,' said Kitty, and as I reluctantly put on my dry set of clothes, Kitty changed into hers. The breeches were baggy and hung halfway down my calves and the sleeves of the shirt were much too long for me.

'Oh, very smart,' she said when we turned around. 'You look a proper Little Lord Fauntleroy.' I didn't know

How embarrassing!

who this little lord was, but it didn't sound much like a compliment. I took my trainers out of my rucksack and slipped them back on. Kitty had put on a pair of trousers and a small jacket and they fitted her perfectly. 'Do you feel any warmer?' she asked, and I had to admit that I did.

Then Kitty took a tin from inside the cupboard and with a knife she wore on her hip, pierced the top and expertly opened it.

'Do you like peaches?' she asked and handed me the tin. I was really hungry and stuffed my mouth full of the slippery, syrupy slices.

'Save some for me!' Kitty protested.

'Sorry,' I mumbled, my mouth still full.

'Now, we'd better work out how to release Dad from the tower,' said Kitty, wiping her hands on her trousers. 'I know the way to the door at the bottom of the stairs, but it's sure to be guarded. That's why I didn't suggest coming this way in the first place.'

'Yes, and the door to the tower is locked and Craik keeps the only key on a string around his neck,' I said.

'There's only one thing we can do then,' said Kitty. 'We'll have to wait until dark and take the key from Craik while he's sleeping. Then we'll have to work out how to get past the guard and into the tower.'

'You must be joking,' I said. 'What if Craik wakes up? We'll be mincemeat.'

'Let's hear your plan then,' said Kitty, but try as I might, I couldn't think of a better one.

'OK, we'll give it a go,' I said, already starting to feel nervous. I'd burgled Craik once when I was a mindless marionette and I'd very nearly been blasted into the middle of next week.

We settled down to wait until dark, but a few minutes later we heard a noise coming from Craik's study and we both stood on the chair and listened through the stuffed head.

(See my journal The Puppet Master's Prison)

Craik Plans

'You useless bunch of drongoes,' Craik bellowed. 'We had them trapped in the moat and you let them slip through your fingers.'

'You too!' said Ham, without thinking.

'What did you say?' spat Craik, staring fiercely at him from under a beetling brow with his one cold, dark eye and one milky, blank one. 'Don't ever back-chat me, you lump of lard,' he hissed and held Ham's gaze until the large, ruddy-faced man looked down at the floor.

'Sorry, boss, sorry for losin' them, boss,' Ham muttered, completely kowtowed.

'That's more like it,' he said. 'Don't ever forget who the boss is around here, or I'll throw you from the top of the tower, just to see if you bounce.'

'OK, boss,' said Ham, backing away like a scolded schoolboy.

'Who was that girl with Charlie, anyway?' asked Twitch, trying to change the subject. 'Why on earth has she been dressing up as a hawk and interfering with our plans?'

'I reckon I know,' chipped in Belcher, pointing at a painting on the wall. 'See the resemblance?'

'Flamin' cannons, you're right,' gasped Craik, going over to the family portrait of a young girl about ten years old and reading the label. 'It's the Squire's daughter. She's come to rescue him. Right, that's decided it. I can't wait for the Squire to sign those deeds now. We'll have to forge his signature and then throw him in the mire. That way there'll be no trace of him.'

'Good idea, boss; I reckon we should've done it a long time ago,' said Belcher.

'You won't mind doin' the dastardly deed then, Belcher,' said Craik. 'First thing in the morning, while the mist is still thick on the ground, take him out and dispose of him. Then, while Twitch and Ham stay here to look after our legal estate, you can join me on a little foray into a new world.' He picked up my map and jabbed it with a rough forefinger. 'Here's where the crossing is. We'll slip into Charlie's world, rob a bank and escape back here. We'll disappear as thoroughly as phantoms and we can go back as many times as we like. It'll be like taking candy from a baby.'

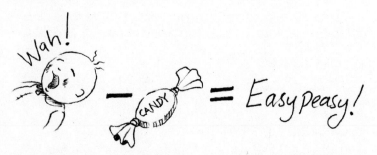

'Perfect,' said Belcher, cracking his knuckles. 'I can't wait.'

'Right, let's go and get some grub,' said Craik with a satisfied look on his ugly mug. 'You're guarding the tower tonight, Twitch. We don't want our bird flying the coop at the last minute, do we?'

'Oh, you know I hate guarding in the dark,' whined Tristram Twitch. 'It's so spooky and I'm sure this place is haunted.'

'Don't be such a wuss!' said Craik. With that, he folded up my map, shoved it inside his shirt and then the whole lot of them stomped out of the room and along the corridor towards the dining room.

'Walt, where's our dinner?' Craik bellowed.

I looked at Kitty. Her face was white with rage. 'We've got to save Dad tonight, Charlie, or it'll be too late.'

'Don't worry, Kit,' I said. 'We'll save him and we'll get rid of the crooks too!' But I had no idea how we were going to do it.

I've just finished writing up my journal. We've been waiting in this little room for hours, but it'll soon be dark and we can sneak upstairs to try to steal the tower key from Craik. I've been going over and over things in my mind and I think I've got the beginnings of a plan; but we're going to have to be as quiet as mice wearing bedroom slippers if we're to get out of this situation in one piece. Wish me luck, and I'll write more as soon as I can.

As Quiet As Mice shhh!

When we heard the grandfather clock in Craik's study chime midnight, Kitty pressed a little brass button and two whole panels in the wall swung silently inwards on hidden hinges. We were level with the top of the mantelpiece over the study's large fireplace, and on one of the swinging doors was the Demon of Darkmoor's snarling head.

'Just a mo',' I whispered, and, taking the megashark's tooth from my explorer's kit, I gave the head a swift thump. The vile thing came away from the plaque and dropped into my hands.

'What are you playing at?' asked Kitty, getting quite

I knocked the head off

stroppy. 'This is no time for souvenir hunting, and anyway, that's Dad's!'

'Sorry, but I've got a feeling it might come in useful,' I said. We jumped down from the mantelpiece into the study and tiptoed across the thick carpet to the door. I peered around the corner to find the hall empty and in darkness.

'All clear,' I whispered and we darted over to the bottom of the wide, sweeping staircase. I secreted the beast's head inside a fancy vase that stood on the end pilaster of one of the banisters.

'Dumping it already? That was a waste of time,' whispered Kitty angrily.

Just then we heard a loud creak coming from the landing above and we both froze, straining our ears. We waited in the eerie darkness, but nothing more happened and eventually we went on. I followed Kitty up the stairs and onto the landing.

'I don't know which is Craik's room, so we'll have to try them all,' said Kitty, her mouth right up against my ear.

A domed skylight above us let in a grey, misty light from the moon and we could see a line of doors stretching both ways down the corridor that ran across the back of the landing.

It's mainly bathrooms and airing cupboards that way,' whispered Kitty and led me along the corridor in the other direction.

She stepped carefully, but even so the floorboards creaked and complained under our weight, sounding very loud in the still night. When the grandfather clock below struck quarter-past the hour, I nearly jumped out of my skin and only just managed to save a little ornament I knocked from its perch in a niche in the wall.

Kitty gripped the handle of the first door and pushed it silently open. The room rumbled to the sound of loud snores and I could make out the huge form of Belcher in the bed underneath a large window.

'Wrong one,' said Kitty, but I pushed past her and stepped into the room.

'Just wait a minute,' I said.

'What now?' she sighed in exasperation.

I tiptoed over to the end of Belcher's bed where his gun belt was draped over a post. I took off my rucksack and groped around inside and then pulled out the bag of marbles and my new glue pen. I squeezed a dollop of glue over the marble and then carefully dropped it down the barrel of Belcher's gun. Now he would get a real surprise when he came to fire it!

We left the room and went on to the next. This was being shared by more of the crook's goons: Syd and Perce, Mad McKay, Sidekick and Gomez. They were snoring so loudly I didn't have to try and be quiet as I booby-trapped their weapons. I did the same to Horatio Ham's gun, dropping a glue-smeared marble into the muzzle, before we finally came to Joseph Craik's bedroom.

A Bit Of Burglary

We slipped into Craik's room. It was as quiet as a grave and I was worried he wasn't there, but as I got closer to the bed I saw his stubbly head on the pillow, his mouth set in a cruel sneer even in sleep. As Kitty fixed his gun with my marbles and glue, I reached with shaking hands for the key that I could see strung around his neck.

I was just about to grab it when he suddenly sat bolt upright with his eyes wide open. I heard Kitty gasp in absolute terror.

'Who goes there?' he growled and I froze with fear as he grabbed my wrist in a vice-like grip. I expected him to leap out of bed and take me prisoner, but he didn't move. Then I realized he was still fast asleep and in the middle of a tumultuous dream. 'I'll get that Charlie Small,' he mumbled. 'I'll get him and I'll, I'll . . .' then with a sigh he let go of my wrist, closed his sightless eyes, collapsed back on the pillow and rolled over.

I breathed again, but when I reached for the key I found it was now wedged firmly under his shoulder. At least he had revealed a corner of a piece of paper sticking out from under his pillow. I grabbed the end and gradually, noiselessly, pulled it free. Yes! It was my precious, priceless map, and I quickly stuffed it in my back pocket.

With the mini-scissor accessory on my multi-tool penknife, I reached forward and snipped the string around Craik's neck. Then, as little beads of cold sweat trickled between my shoulder blades, I took his warty nose between

my thumb and forefinger and gently
turned his head.

'Wasshappenin'?' he
moaned in his sleep, but it
worked – Craik rolled right
over and I immediately
snatched the key, let go of his
nose and backed towards the door where Kitty
was waiting for me. I slipped through the gap
and we closed the door silently behind us, as we
both let out a rush of air.

'Phewee!' I gasped. 'I thought we'd had it
then.'

'Me too!' said Kitty, with a nervous giggle
in her voice. Then we both started giggling
uncontrollably, desperately trying to muffle our
sniggers.

'Shush!' I managed to say, my shoulders
shuddering with stifled mirth – and then we
both started again.

Eventually our giggling subsided and, taking
a deep breath, Kitty said, 'Come on, time is
cracking on. Let's get to the tower.'

'Before we do, can you show me a linen
cupboard?' I asked.

'What the heck . . . Oh, I suppose you have

The key!

your reasons,' said Kitty, looking at me as if I was mad. 'This way.'

We crept along to the other end of the corridor where she opened two large cupboard doors, revealing shelves stacked with sheets, tablecloths and clothes. I grabbed a folded sheet and put it under my arm.

'Thanks,' I said. 'Come on, let's go.'

'You are weird,' muttered Kitty, shaking her head as we retraced our steps.

A Haunting We Will Go!

At the bottom of the stairs, I retrieved the Demon's head and followed Kitty as she tiptoed along the wide corridor that led away from the back of the massive entrance hall.

We went past a meeting room, a trophy room, a stateroom, the ballroom and the kitchens before turning and hurrying through the dining room.

Blimey, this place is ginormous! I thought. The dining table was a jumble of dirty plates, spilled wine glasses and half-finished food. Beyond, the passage became narrower and was much windier.

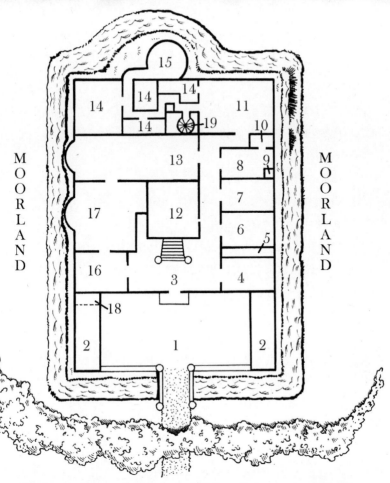

Groundfloor Plan of Hawksmoor Hall

1) Courtyard
2) Stables
3) Main Hall
4) Study
5) Secret Room
6) Meeting Room
7) Trophy Room
8) Kitchen
9) Entrance To Cellar
10) Pantry
11) Dining Room
12) Stateroom
13) Ballroom
14) Store and Lumber Rooms
15) Tower
16) Library
17) Lounge
18) Walt's Room
19) Back Stairs

Now we were amongst the lumber rooms and storerooms. As we approached a ninety-degree turn in the corridor, Kitty held up her hand for me to stop. We crept forward and she peered round the corner.

'Just as we thought – he's there,' she whispered. I looked round and saw Twitch at the far end of the passage, guarding a locked door with the word TOWER carved into it. He was sitting in a chair, staring through the gloom with wide, scared eyes and holding a pistol in hands that were shaking like leaves on a tree.

'There's no such thing as ghosts,' he was saying over and over to himself. 'There's no such thing as ghosts; there's no such thing as ghosts.'

'What do we do now?' whispered Kitty.

'Just you watch,' I said, tying the sheet around my neck so that it hung down to the floor. Then, fitting the Demon's head over mine like a horrific Halloween mask, I stepped round the corner emitting a series of low guttural growls.

'Wh- wh- wh- wh- who goes there?' stammered Twitch as I

Grrrr!

It's the Demon's ghost!

slowly marched towards him. Then he let out an ear-piercing scream that echoed along the passage. 'Oh my giddy aunt, it's the Demon of Darkmoor's ghost. Eeeek! He's come back to haunt the manor.' He dropped his pistol and as it hit the hard floor it went off.

PTANG! A bullet whizzed past my ear and ricocheted off the wall as Tristram Twitch, his legs reduced to jelly, flopped to the ground in a dead faint.

'OK, Kitty, he's out cold,' I said, taking off the Demon's head and the sheet and dropping them on the floor. 'Let's get a move on.'

As Kitty raced to join me, I unlocked the door and swung it wide open. Then, taking the ball of string from my explorer's kit, I tied Twitch up and we dragged him into the tower, leaning him up against the wall at the base of the spiral stairs.

'Let's go,' I said, closing the door behind us and then racing up the stairs behind my friend.

Four hundred steps later, we reached the top, puffing and wheezing like ancient steam engines.

'Dad, wake up!' cried Kitty as I unlocked the door to his cell. 'We're here to rescue you.'

'Who's that?' came a querulous voice as the

door swung open. Caught in a strong beam of moonlight from the slit windows, the Squire was sitting up in bed with the bedclothes pulled right up to his eyes, peering at us with fear and dread.

'Dad, it's me, Kitty! Come on, do!' said the girl.

Well, the Squire was out of bed in a second. He ran over to his daughter and took her by the hand, spinning her round in a madcap dance, his nightshirt flapping against his skinny legs.

'I'm free, haha, I'm free, haha, I'm free, I'm free, I'm free!' he started to gabble maniacally.

'Calm down, Dad, everything's going to be OK,' said Kitty, looking concerned at the state of her overwrought father. 'I think he's gone a little doolally,' she whispered, turning to me.

'Don't worry, he'll soon be his old self,' I reassured her, but at that moment he looked as crazy as a cuckoo!

'This is not the time for dancing, Dad,' said Kitty firmly. 'We've got to go.'

A minute later, the Squire was fully dressed and much calmer, and a minute after that we were at the bottom of the tower steps. Twitch

was still out cold and we stepped over him
into the corridor. As we did so, Belcher came
lumbering around the corner like a huge bull, his
mean little eyes shining from under the pattern
of tattoos on his wedge-nosed fizzog.

Fight! Kerpow!

'Oh my, Charlie, what have *you* come as – Little
Lord Fauntleroy?' he chuckled when he saw
what I was wearing, his corpulent body shaking
like a massive jelly.

'Ha, ha! What have you come as – a great
ape?' I retorted.

'Unlucky for you, dear boy, but this great ape
is a very light sleeper,' he said.

It's the only light thing about you, I thought as my
heart sank.

'I heard a pistol shot and came to investigate
and it looks like I've caught the whole bad lot
of you together. Craik is going to be as pleased
as punch. Come on, you're coming with me.'
He pulled the pistol from his belt to cover us,
but the thought of being recaptured so quickly
made the Squire completely lose his head.

'You great, lumbering loser,' he said, pushing past me and marching straight towards the brigand.

'Dad!' cried Kitty.

'Back, buster,' cried Belcher, shocked at the Squire's boldness. I'm not sure he meant to fire it, but somehow Belcher's pistol went off. There was an enormous bang as the blocked barrel exploded and the brigand dropped the weapon. 'Jeepers!' he yelled, clutching his hand. 'That flamin' hurts!' Then, recovering himself, he stared at us malevolently. 'Right, you're for it now,' he sneered and still nursing his throbbing hand, strode towards us.

'Gangway!' cried Kitty and in two athletic leaps she flew down the corridor, span like a top in mid-air and delivered a crunching karate chop to Belcher's neck. The blubbery brigand crumpled to the floor with a wheezing sigh.

'Kitty, where on earth did you learn to do that?' gasped the Squire.

'Miss Prim's Academy,' said Kitty with a huge grin.

'But it's meant to teach you to be a young lady,' complained her dad.

'Being a demure young damsel wouldn't have knocked out this great goon, would it, Dad?' said Kitty. 'Right, give us a hand, you two.'

Together we dragged the brigand along the corridor and into the room at the bottom of the tower. It took all our strength – it was like trying to move a beached whale! We propped him up next to Twitch and I tied him tight with my ball of twine. Then, locking the door behind us, we scarpered along the passage.

We had made a lot of noise and now we could hear lots of scurrying footsteps. Some of Craik's cronies had been roused and were on our trail.

'Uh-oh!' said Kitty. 'We have company.'

As we ran into the hall, some of the crooks were rushing down the main staircase.

'We've got the varmints,' crowed Ham. Then, 'Whoa!' he cried as he lost his footing and his great frame tumbled heavily down the stairs. His thick head landed with a crack on the marble floor and he was knocked out cold.

'Stop right there,' yelled Mad Marshall Mickey McKay as he raised his pistol and fired a warning shot in the air. Kerboom! The booby-trapped gun exploded. 'Yeowza!' bellowed the Marshall, clutching his hand and then rushing off to plunge it under a running tap.

Syd and Perce saw what had happened, peered down the barrels of their guns and threw them to the ground.

'Been up to your old tricks have you, Charlie Small?' grunted Syd, grabbing a mace from a nearby suit of armour and swinging it through the air. As the two bull-necked bouncers advanced towards us, Kitty flew at Syd.

'Hi-*ya!*' she cried, side-stepping the flying mace as Syd brought it swishing towards her again and again.

'I'll squash you like a fly!' he roared, but with a flurry of kicks and slaps she stunned the bully senseless. *Crack, bash, bang, wallop!*

'Go, Kitty, go!' cried the Squire as Syd crumpled to the floor in a heap.

Perce took a sword from the wall and ran at me. I reached for my scimitar and then remembered I'd left it back at the Hawk's Nest. *Darn it!*

'Here, Charlie,' cried the Squire, taking a sword from a suit of armour and throwing it to me. I caught it by the handle and turned to face Perce. He grinned a menacing grin and swished his sword through the air threateningly.

Now, I don't like to boast, but an expert taught me to swordfight and I could tell that Perce, despite all his posturing, was an amateur. With a few swift strokes I sent his sword flying through the air. I backed him into a chair where he sat down heavily and the Squire brought a metal shield down on his head with a clang.

'Take that you no-good, low-down, dirty dog,' he cried as Kitty tied the unconscious bandit tight with a bell-pull she'd ripped from the ceiling.

Finally, Craik himself appeared on the landing with Gomez and Sidekick, the two remaining members of his gang.

'Charlie Small, I might have known it'd be you disturbing my beauty sleep,' he growled. 'Let's get 'em, men.' They ran towards the top of the stairs just as Walt appeared through the front door from his sleeping quarters in the stables. Everyone ignored him as he rubbed his eyes dozily and shuffled across the hall in a pair of outsized slippers.

'Is it mornin'?' he asked in his slow drawl, reaching the foot of the stairs just as Craik came bounding down.

'Out of my way, you gormless yokel,' cried Craik, trying to barge past. Then, 'Whoa!' he cried, tripping over Walt's foot and crashing to the hard, marble floor.

'Whoops, sorry?' chuckled Walt as my pals and I ran for the front door.

'You did that on purpose, you idiotic slowcoach!' cried Craik.

'Let me help you up,' said the canny Moor's Man, reaching down for the struggling gang boss and purposely getting in his way.

'You nincompoop!' cried Craik, taking out his pistol. 'I'll blast you to kingdom come!' He aimed the gun and fired. His pistol exploded. *BOOM!*

'Missed?' said Walt with a grin.

'Blue blazes!' cried Craik, flapping his hand

as if he were waving us goodbye; he looked so comical, we couldn't help but laugh.

'I'll get you for this, Charlie Small!' he bellowed, but I had one more trick up my sleeve. I grabbed the smoke bombs from my rucksack and as we reached the main entrance, I lobbed them back into the room.

Mayhem On The Moor

We careered across the courtyard as smoke billowed from the doors. As we crossed the bridge and dashed along the tree-lined tunnel, we could hear the crooks' hacking coughs and curses as they bumped into each other in the confusion.

We dashed across the crop fields and leaped over drainage ditches like Olympic athletes. The Squire was remarkably fast for such a chubby chap and kept up with us easily. The sky was already starting to lighten as dawn approached and the moor mist lay thick on the ground.

Beyond the fields we clambered up the slope to the top of the ridge where Nightmare was waiting. He could smell the excitement in the air and was pawing the ground impatiently with his hooves, snorting loudly and shaking his long mane.

Kitty leaped onto Nightmare's back and I pushed the Squire up behind her. Now we could hear the thunder of horses' hooves from below and, peering through the weak dawn light, I made out Craik, Sidekick and Gomez in the mist. They had saddled their horses and were galloping over the fields.

'Time to go,' said Kitty, kicking Nightmare into a gallop. 'See you back at the Hawk's Nest, Charlie,' she cried over her shoulder before disappearing in the fog.

'No problem,' I replied. I picked up the Air-rider and pressed the start button. Nothing happened. I pressed it again – still nothing. *Oh, please don't fail me now,* I thought, starting to panic as the pounding hooves drew nearer. I gave the scooter a shake and tried once more. It started, and I leaped onto the footplate, twisted the accelerator grip and raced away.

Glancing over my shoulder, I noticed that Gomez and Sidekick had broken away from Craik and were racing away to my left.

They're trying to cut off my escape route, I thought and turned my scooter the other way. But the two crooks kept galloping in the opposite direction and I realized they had decided to cut their losses and bail out.

'Come back, you snivelling creeps,' Craik

yelled after them, but they carried on and were soon lost to sight. 'It's just you and me now Charlie,' he cried. 'Just like old times!'

'So long, sucker!' I yelled and opened the Air-rider up to top speed. I whizzed over the moor, holding on tight as the uneven ground started to make the machine judder. The swirling mist grew thicker and soon it was hard to see further than ten metres.

'You can run, but you can't hide,' came Craik's reply as I started to leave him behind. 'You might as well just hand back the map right now.'

You've gotta be joking, I thought, but as I turned to look over my shoulder, the scooter hit a large stone hidden in the fog. *Thump!* 'Yikes!' I cried and went somersaulting over the handlebars, landing with a bump on the springy grass. I scrambled to my feet and dashed back to my scooter, but Craik was already on me.

With a whoop of delight he pulled his panting horse to a stop and leaped to the ground. I raced away over the moor. He was after me in an instant as I ran through the mist, turning this way and that, not knowing which way to go and hardly able to see the ground in front of me. Then, when I heard a splash and felt thick, cold mud seep into my trainers, I knew I'd made a stupendous blunder. I tried to pull my feet free, but the sticky mud sucked them down further. Oh, yikes! I had run straight into a quagmire.

'Help!' I cried, as Craik casually walked towards me and sat on a rock at the edge of the bog. He grasped his bony knees with his rough hands, and with his shoulders hunched up around his ears he looked like a malevolent old crow.

'Oh, so you've found Gloopen Mire, have you?' he said with an evil smile. 'It looks like it's finally all over, Charlie,'

'It is for you,' I said, my legs sinking deeper into the mud. 'The Squire has escaped and your gang is either knocked out cold, locked up or they've scarpered. You might as well clear out whilst you still have the chance.' The mire gave a loud gurgle and I felt the sticky mud rise over my knees and up my thighs.

'Brave words from a boy waist deep in a

malodorous mire,' sighed Craik. 'But you're right, it's getting more trouble than it's worth around here and it's time I moved on. The only way you'll be going though, is down!'

'You mean you'd let me sink into this slime?' I cried.

'It'll save me a hanging – unless, no . . .'

'What?' I cried as, with a bubbling of mud, I sank up to my chest.

'Nothing,' said Craik casually.

'Tell me,' I pleaded.

'Unless you hand over that map, of course,' said Craik, nonchalantly examining his fingernails.

I thought about it. It would be a terrible blow, but it would be better than a muddy grave. 'OK, you've got a deal,' I said, reaching into my back pocket and, with some difficulty, forcing my arm out of the mud. 'Here, take it.'

Craik leaned forward and plucked the precious map from my fingers. 'Thanks, Charlie,' he said. Then, checking he'd got the genuine article, he turned to go.

'Hey, what about me?' I cried, but the dastardly fiend just laughed and waved goodbye.

Oh no! I was being abandoned!

Big Bertha!

All of a sudden I could hear a slow *clump, clump, clump,* as if a large animal was stomping across the moor in slow motion. Craik stopped in his tracks and looked puzzled. In front of him, about fifty Moor's Folk stepped ponderously out of the mist. They looked like spectres with their long, pale green faces and they were all carrying makeshift weapons; pitchforks, spades, ladles and potato peelers.

'Get out of my way, you pea-brained peasants,' growled Craik, nervously.

'I'll take that map, thank you,' said the Squire, stepping from amongst the crowd with Kitty by his side.

Hurry up, I thought, trying to stay afloat. *Or the earth's going to swallow me whole!*

'Oh, clear off, loony,' said Craik trying to sound confident, but taking a step backwards nonetheless. All signs of the Squire's panicky nervousness had gone though, and he raised a large, trumpet-shaped rifle to his shoulder.

'Meet Big Bertha, my great granddaddy's trusty old blunderbuss,' he said. 'It saw to the Demon of Darkmoor and it can do the same to

Meet Big Bertha!

you. So hand over Charlie's map right now.'

'No way,' said Craik, looking around for an escape route.

Hurry up, I'm sinking! I thought as the mud settled just below my chin.

BABOOM! A mighty explosion echoed across the moor as the Squire let off Big Bertha. 'I'm not joking,' he said.

Me neither, I silently yelled inside my head. *Hurry up!*

With an angry sneer, Craik screwed up the map and threw it on the ground. 'Have it if you want,' he spat.

'Now get off my moor and never show your ugly mug in these parts again,' said the Squire. 'Go on, my nerves are still all of a flutter and this thing might go off at any minute.'

'Yeah, get lost?' cried one of the Moor's Men

and with that the whole crowd started banging and rattling their weapons together, advancing slowly towards the crook.

'OK, OK. I know where I'm not wanted,' Craik said nervously, and climbed onto his horse. Then, looking down at me, he said, 'You haven't seen the last of me, Charlie Small. Just watch your back.' With that he urged his horse into a gallop and disappeared into the morning mist.

'Hooray? Hip, hip hooray?' the crowd yelled.

'Mmm, mmmm, mm!' I cried, unable to open my mouth for fear of having it filled with mud.

'Coming, Charlie,' cried Kitty, unravelling a long rope she had wound across her shoulders. 'We haven't forgotten you!'

I was up to my neck in trouble!

An hour later I was warming myself in front of a roaring fire in the Squire's study, after a hot, soapy bath. All the remaining crooks had been locked in the room at the top of the tower while the Squire decided what to do with them, and I could smell the delicious aroma of frying bacon and sausages coming from the kitchens.

The Squire seemed quite back to normal now he was free and in his own home once more. He sat at the desk, leaning back in his chair with his hands behind his head and a beaming smile on his face.

'You must stay with us, Charlie,' he said. 'It's the least we can do after all you've done to help us. I'll raise you as my own son and you'll have the best of everything. Just think what larks we could have, you and me.'

'Yes, please stay, it'll be great fun,' said Kitty. She looked quite different now, dressed in a long, pretty yellow gown. 'Perhaps you could go to a school like mine. And in the holidays we could race our horses across the moors and go hunting for deadly Darkmoor Demons!'

'It sounds great,' I said. 'But I really have to get home.' I looked at my mud-splattered map for the umpteenth time. 'I've still got a long way to go and Mum is expecting me home for tea.'

'Well, if you're quite sure,' said the Squire, as Walt appeared to announce that breakfast was ready.

'Yeah, I'm quite sure, thanks,' I said. 'I'll set off first thing tomorrow.

'Well, just remember you'll always find a welcome home here, my boy.'

Towards Home!

I'm in the foothills of the range of mountains that my map calls the Jagged Edge. They are enormous and stretch right across the horizon, their peaks lost among the clouds. Behind me the moor is glowing gold in the late afternoon sun.

The air is as clear as crystal and I can see for

miles and miles. I can't see a solitary figure, but I've got the strangest feeling I'm not alone. I've had this feeling ever since I left Hawksmoor Hall, two days ago.

I spent a lazy and restful last day with Kitty and her dad, and the following morning, after some long goodbyes, I drove my Air-rider down the drive, my scimitar hanging from my waist. All the moor folk had come to wish me well and were lined up on either side of the gravel drive, waving and cheering. It quite choked me up.

As soon as I was on the open moor though, the feeling started to creep over me that I was being followed and I felt nervous and edgy. Every now and then, I'd spin round and check the landscape behind me, but apart from flickering shadows that might have come from the scudding clouds in the sky, and the sound of the sharp wind that cut across the downs, I didn't see or hear anything.

Now, from my vantage point in the hills, I am scanning the moorland with my telescope. *There!* I'm sure I saw a movement among the raised stones of a Tor. Now it's gone again. Am I imagining things, or is Craik keeping his promise and trailing my every move?

The only thing I can do is keep on moving. I'll make my way into the mountains and find a safe place for the night. I have a rucksack bursting with grub and know where I'm bound. I'm heading straight for the massive sprawl of Fortune City, halfway between here and my final destination – the secret way back into my own world.

Who knows what frightful dangers await me before I get there! What sort of dreadful creatures might live in the mountains or on the Great Waste? My skin is getting goose-pimples just thinking about it! Whatever happens, I will write everything down in my journal of adventures.

Wish me luck!

PUBLISHER'S NOTE

This is where Charlie's eleventh journal ends. Will he make it to the hidden bridge between our two worlds; is Joseph Craik really on his trail; if Charlie does make it home, will his tea be ready for him? Keep your eyes peeled for another fantastic Charlie Small journal!

www.charliesmall.co.uk

Ugly blighter!
CRAIK
Bubbling bog!
Don't call me Just a girl!
I won, I won and, I lost, I lost!

LOOK out!
Who wants a crispy, gooey bug? Yum, yum!
The Squire
Tristram Twitch
There's no such thing as ghosts!
Follow, follow
Charlie Small
Charlie Small
Charlie Small

follow, follow, follow the thin red line!
Little Lord Fauntleroy
At last I'm going home!
Is Craik still on my trail?

The Hawk!